D0878270

THE
BADLANDS
Fox

by
Margaret Lemley Warren

Edited by
Renée Sansom Flood

Margaret Lemley Warren
9/8/91

THE BADLANDS FOX

For further information:
Margaret Lemley Warren
Rt. 2 Box 49A
Hermosa, SD 57744

FIRST EDITION

Library of Congress Catalog Card Number 91-92834
ISBN: 0-913062-00-6

Pa in the saddle at Belle Fourche.

TABLE OF CONTENTS

AUTHOR'S NOTE

I salute Beverly Pehan, who goaded me into this adventure, and my editor, Renee Sansom Flood, who is as tense as a hen on a hot griddle. Many thanks to Eka Parkison and Oliver Bradford for helping Renee with research, to friends Shane Taylor, Butch Conrad, and Dayton Hyde for encouragement when the goin' got rough, and to my nephew, William R. Lemley Sr. for the historic photographs.

Many people contributed their time but I would especially like to thank my beloved cousin Margaret Morgan Hawkins, who at ninety years of age gave me my mother's poignant letters. And I won't forget Herman Bloom who labored to bring Pa's ranch through WWII and listened to these anecdotes a jillion times!

Thanks to beautiful Evangeline Matta Morgan who transcribed five sides of very noisy tapes, almost an impossible feat. And thanks to friends Laverne and Hokie Andersen, and to Walter Maude for taking the time to help remember Pa.

Mae and Marvin Maude took over the ranch and fed my animals so that I could recuperate from Shingles in peace. They even went shopping, hauled groceries, and fixed machinery! My eternal gratitude to all my genuine and kindly neighbors on Spring Creek who have helped me at every turn of the road since I bought my first ranch in 1962, and to "Big Chuck" Strehlow, my father's good friend, and mine.

With great warmth I acknowledge a debt of gratitude to my cousin Larry Lemley, DVM, who copied Pa's tapes that my long-suffering brother was reluctant to give me...he (brother Ray) was afraid I might do something bizarre like...write a book!

Margaret Lemley Warren
June 1, 1991

CALAMITY JANE

Pete Lemley, a fifteen year-old daredevil with a sparkle in his eye, decided he was going to buy Calamity Jane a beer! The handsome young man and his friend Jack Dawson set their sights on rip-roaring Deadwood, the most lawless, brawling mining camp on the 1885 Dakota frontier. Like other lads, Pa had heard about the adventures of Calamity Jane, Buffalo Bill and Deadwood Dick, incredible characters any boy would love to meet. Calamity or Marthy Canary, alias Somers, King, Dorsett, Hunt, Hickok, Steers, Dalton, Wilson, Washburn, Coombs, Buck, and Burke was a real-life renegade, A whoop-up bull whackeress if ever there was one. She lived in Deadwood from time to time and most folks couldn't decide whether she was a low-down prostitute, (a soiled dove) or an angel of mercy, both qualities she displayed during Dakota's raunch-iest territorial days.

Bumming on the rails all the way from Russell, Iowa, Pa and his pal Jack took advantage of railroad conductors who conveniently looked the other way. They were on a thrilling adventure and nothin' could stop them, not even the end of the railroad line at Buffalo Gap. Pa never told anyone how he comman-deered horses, (maybe even legally) but in less than two days he rode ninety miles to Deadwood, reinin' up in front of Mike Russell's Saloon lookin' for the noto-rious "star" of many legends.

Pa wasn't a bit shy as he swung open the saloon doors and sauntered up to the honky tonk bar. From somewhere in the back he could hear a piano, glass-es tinkling, cowboys and miners cussing and boasting, spitting and laughing up-roariously, and by golly there she was.

"I knew her quick as I seen her," Pa recalled. Calamity Jane looked over at the pale blue eyes and hooted, "Kid, where'd you come from?" It was then Pa turned on his smooth-talkin' charm, the charm he would use to seduce women the rest of his life, "I come one thousand miles jes' to see you ma'am," he grinned.

"Like hell you did! Kinda young for me aincha' kid?"

Calamity laughed out loud but she was plainly flattered and leaned closer towards Pa to accept the beer he'd been achin' to buy her.

The boys stayed in Deadwood four more days, after all, they might as well look for famed Sheriff Seth Bullock, the man who single-handedly and without a shot being fired, brought Matt Plunkett and his mine robbers to justice. Plunkett, a wily sort, had tried to steal the Hidden Treasure Gulch Mine in the fall of 1877. A violent dispute arose with the owners over wages while Plunkett was foreman. He and the miners rebelled, moved into the tunnel where they were working, and prepared to stay until they got the wages they wanted. The men dragged in beds, bedding, a cook stove, and supplies, settling in like squirrels for the winter. The mine owners legally appealed to Judge Bennett's court and the judge sent Seth Bullock with a posse to dispossess the claim jumpers from the tunnel.

The miners had no respect whatever for the law. They wouldn't even answer Bullock's growling threats at the tunnel entrance. United States troops reinforced the sheriff but they too failed to roust the entrenched miners. Bullock's Montana vigilante blood rose higher and higher. Leaving the posse at the mouth of the tunnel, he climbed the mountain side to the air shaft where smoke was filtering out from a meal the miners were cooking deep in the mine. The crafty sheriff reached over, his long mustache fairly drooping into the shaft and dropped something through the chimney into the fire. Jumping sideways down the mountainside, he reached the mouth of the tunnel just as the miners rushed out holding their noses, eyes streaming, and heads down. Bullock had dropped asafetida into the miners' cookstove and the disgusting smell had driven them out into the hands of the law, one of the only times in the early history of Deadwood that a fierce dispute was settled without bloodshed.

Pa and his friend missed seeing gunslinger Wild Bill Hickok but they got to see the No. Ten Saloon where Jack McCall murdered Hickok in cold blood. They sat out in front to watch the Deadwood stage, even though they couldn't afford to take a ride. The six white horses with nickel-plated trappings pranced and glittered in and out of Deadwood, a romantic sight for two young men stirred with the love of adventure.

Evenings, the boys crossed over Wall Street, the evil path dividing bad from good in Deadwood; below which the police never went after dark. Bawdy saloons caused a general uproar nearly every night. The boys watched, pokin' fun at the fancy jingling spurs and gaudy dressed locals struttin' in and out of town. But the sudden gunshots were not a joking matter; loud and bloody head-bashings that usually started in the saloons, spillin' out into the streets, while lovely soiled doves, ("chippies") watched and beckoned the young men with suggestive taunts. "Deadwood's not that tough; not much worse'n Rapid City; 'bout the same," Pa told his friend.

Four days later, tired, broke, but satisfied, Pa hitched a ride to Buffalo Gap and from there back to Iowa on the rails. It's a safe bet my ornery Pa lost his virginity in Deadwood, although he'd probably already seduced the hired girl when he was nine! Pa always knuckled his mustache and said, "I had the best of it."

JES' KNOCKIN' AROUND

Trailing a herd just east of the Black Hills, the land of adventure, turned out to be a lot more interesting to Pa than pitchin' hay on an Iowa farm. His parents, Jacob and Margaret Bell Lemley had nine children, three boys, Ramsey, Theodore and Pa, and six girls. Jacob originally came from Greenville, Pennsylvania, where his father had migrated from Germany. Jacob and wife lived for a spell in Wheeling, West Virginia and after the Civil War they went west. Later, Jacob drove Longhorns up from Texas, branding them on the horn (with three bars) rather than the hide of later days. The Lemleys moved out upon the great empty land into an awesome world of earth and sky. For some folks the prospect was a world of freedom and beauty but for others it was a frightening, maddening experience.

Jacob bought eight thousand acres from the Burlington Railroad for a dollar and a half an acre. He and his eldest son Ramsey built an oak and hickory log house, fifty feet long and twenty feet wide. "It was tough goin' sometimes; lots of troubles," Pa said. But that didn't keep him from havin' a little boyish fun, huntin' the now extinct passenger pigeons that were so plentiful:

> *They'd break the tree limbs down. We kids used to hunt with a muzzle-loadin' rifle 'bout the size of a thirty-two. We could shoot squirrels outta them trees; we were good shots, been shootin' since we was big enough to walk. We made our own bullets outta caps and powder; the guns were accurate; I could hit anything the size of a dollar from one hundred yards anytime.*

Since money was scarce and there were so many children, Pa despised "eatin' cornmeal with milk three times a day." Maybe that's why he hated cornmeal to the end of his long life.

Jacob and his boys picked corn and hauled it by mule to a Russell, Iowa mill. They traded cornmeal for groceries and never did see any real money except when Jesse James came ridin' up for a meal. Pa consorted with the likes of Jesse James and his crew when he was a lad of ten or twelve years. Since Pa's family

Grandpa Jacob Lemley   1828-1906.

lived near the Missouri border, Jesse and his fellow travelers were once-in-a-while guests for dinner. Jesse was a real gentleman and everybody liked him. He paid for everything he wanted and never threw his weight around. Pa told about the time the James boys held up a bank (probably the Corydon, Iowa bank for $45,000) and then stopped for a meal at his parents' house:

Jesse, Frank, Cole Younger, Charlie Pitts, and another fellow wanted to know if they could get dinner and feed their horses and Ma told them yes, there was some corn fodder there and they fed their horses. She fixed dinner for them. Jesse and Cole was joshing each other about mistakes they had made and one thing and another and they had a big time talkin' and laughin' and when they got through dinner, why Jesse asked how much they owed and she said they never charged anything; they fed everybody who come along. So when they went away Jesse left ten dollars under the plate! And a couple or three hours after that about twenty fellows come along lookin' for 'em. Ma said they asked her a lot of fool questions. . . .She said she didn't know who they was and she would feed anyone who come along. The posse was mad but she didn't think they was trying to catch 'em very hard; didn't want to catch up with 'em.

Even the suspicion that Jesse's cash came from a train or a bank holdup didn't mar the pleasure of spending that money Jesse left for grandma.

One of Pa's favorite stories was about Jesse riding by a modest farm home when he discovered the widowed lady of the house shedding buckets of tears because the banker had just been there and delivered his ultimatum. . ."Pay up, or else!" He was supposed to foreclose the next day but Jesse had a plan. He dried her tears, gave her a fistful of money, and told her to get all the papers signed the next day, releasing the debt after she had paid the banker. She cheered up, thanked her lucky stars, and looked forward to "tomorrow." All went as predicted. The banker arrived, signed the papers, accepted the money, and greedily went on his way. . .but not very far. Jesse bushwacked him and took back his money.

Somehow the people in the area had a real soft spot in their hearts for Jesse. Years later the man who finally shot him damned near lost his neck to the irate public. Poor man, probably congratulating himself on ridding the country of a dangerous criminal and dreaming of praises to come from a grateful populace. He must have been stunned that instead of rewards and fame, he had to run for his life! Pa said the man's name was Ford and he'd always get a faraway look in his eyes when he'd tell of the old days:

I remember it well. The people wanted to go get that damned Ford and hang him! the people around there liked young James. The

The Lemley family. Preston, back row, far right.

Youngers were all right. Cole Younger was 'bout his same kind of fella, but they spoke of Jesse the most. He'd come along to a fella's place and if they had a horse that he liked, he would try to buy him. If he couldn't buy him, he'd go get another horse and trade with 'em, or he would pay a helluva price for the horse. He would never have taken him or nothin', good man to deal with.

In April of 1882, a fly-speck kid named Bob Ford shot Jesse James in the back at his home in St. Joseph, Missouri. While Jesse was standin' on a chair dusting off a portrait of Stonewall Jackson, Ford sneaked up behind him with a nickel-plated revolver Jesse had given him and shot three times, killing the most famous, feared, and well-loved outlaw in American history.

Pa's family ended up in Iowa, migratin' from Jesse James country. He heard many stories about Abe Lincoln while he was growin' up and they were all good ones. None of the family were in the Civil War and it seemed strange to him that abolitionists were so worried about breakin' up black slave families, they just had to go and kill more white American boys than in any other war in history! Take any war, look at the reasons for it, and that's goin' to hold true. Wars are just another way to line the pockets of businessmen when business hasn't been too good.

Pa's folks weren't the warring kind. There was too much work just makin' a livin' from day to day. They butchered their own animals, cured the meat, ground up cane and made molasses by boiling it in big boxes with tin bottoms. Pa often told about the hard work: "splittin' rails out of oak trees to build fences; stake and rider fences they called them. They'd run the corners zig-zag, run 'em out and lay 'em on each others' end, you see. It would take twice as much fence as if they'd been laid out straight." Jacob's father came over from Germany and his wife's people were from Scotland. They all were used to hard work and long days. In fact, it was all constant toil, little play, no wages or pocket money, and too damned many kids! Pa didn't want a monotonous, treadmill life. The tales of gold diggin' and living a little more adventurous got to him and the next thing you know, he was on the bum again, itchin' for some excitement.

President Grover Cleveland, the big, good-humored man called "Uncle Jumbo" by his relatives, was in the White House and the latest fad was the bicycle when Pa started north on the rails in 1888. Old Cleveland shocked a few people when he married twenty-one year old Frances Folsom, making her the youngest first lady in history, but he was a hard-workin' man so people forgave him for robbing the cradle. One of his cronies grumbled that Cleveland would "rather do something badly for himself than have somebody else do it well." In 1888, Benjamin Harrison was elected president but Cleveland vowed to return. When Mrs. Cleveland left the White House she turned to the servants and said, "I want you to take good care of all the furniture and ornaments in the house, for I want to find everything just as it is now when we come back again . . . four

Pete Lemley and brother Theodore in 1890.

years from today." Sure enough, the American public soon grew tired of Harrison's extravagant spending habits and Mrs. Cleveland came back when she said she would. Not long afterward, Cleveland was secretly operated on for cancer of the mouth and had to wear an artificial jaw made of rubber for the rest of his life. Most presidents don't have Cleveland's excuse to keep jawin'.

People said the era of the western frontier was drawin' to a close but nobody in Dakota Territory would have believed that! This time when Pa headed north he had to pay special attention to the bouncers hired to throw hoboes, greenhorns, and drunks off trains if they were bumming rides. Hoboes were a vinegar sort—a collection of men as hard-boiled as twenty-minute eggs and as irresponsible and shiftless as the summer winds. They traveled the country carrying no water, blankets, or money, because the money they did earn soon went for cards, liquor, and joy girls. Drunks were everywhere. Western writer Hamlin Garland described the men as "arriving like a flight of alien unclean birds, and vanished into the north as mysteriously as they had appeared . . ." They had a slang term of their own and called each other "Bo," a contraction for "Boy." In time they were called "H'o Bos" which meant "Hello, boy"—a greeting of one stranger to another when they met on the trail.

Pa had to sleep and eat right next to hoboes, lousy, rancid-smellin' men, on his way to Hot Springs, South Dakota, a pretty little town smack in the middle of what he called, "God's Country." Pa brought along another friend and when the two arrived in town it was just noon and they were hungry. All they had between them was seventy cents, so they decided they, "jes" as well be broke as to have only seventy cents! They treated themselves to a five course dinner for thirty-five cents including a glass of beer. Pa always maintained that, "Hot Springs ruined its chances to be really big. The travelin' men got all riled up when they raised the price of a five-course meal from twenty-five cents to thirty-five cents!"

Leaning against a wooden porch railing afterward, contentedly picking their teeth, they witnessed a heated argument right out in front. Two men were havin' at it, cussing and beating on each other until one of them, the driver of a big mule team, was fired on the spot. Not one to let the dust settle on a new idea, Pa jumped down from the porch and struck while the iron was hot. He asked for the job. The foreman looked him up and down and had a hard time deciding whether he should give such a young man all that responsibility. He couldn't afford to be too choosy because there just wasn't anybody else around. "You're a mite young to be handlin' all them mules, kid," he grumbled, but Pa persisted. They were building an elegant hotel in Hot Springs and imported Italians were cutting huge blocks of sandstone for the walls. The foreman needed someone who could break wild mules, a mule skinner's job. "I know I can," says Pa, jumping on the back of the lead mule as agile and fast as a monkey. "You have a week to break 'em and I'll give you thirty dollars a month and board. Do you want anybody to help you?" the foreman snapped sarcastically. "I don't need any help," Pa told his new boss. "All's I need are some halters, a set of harness and one gentle mule." The mules were named Wild Bill and Victoria and they couldn't do nothin' with 'em:

By nine o'clock that night, I had those two tied together and the harness on. I had old Victoria with her foot tied up, and I was standin' on top of her playing with her ears. That night the boss come down and told me if I could make a good team outta those mules, he'd give me fifty dollars a month, good wages for those times. All them old-timers was gettin' only thirty dollars. When I finished that job and he paid me off the boss says, "You made me more money than any of these men I've got, or any man I ever hired. Those mules wasn't worth a penny when you took ahold of 'em and now I could sell 'em for five hundred dollars!

It was the beginning of many legends about Pa's genius with livestock. Breakin' mules came easy and fellas used to ask him how he did it:

Well, I attached my rope to the top of the big, freight wheels and dug a loop and run it past them, caught 'em and they went to the end of the rope and I throwed 'em. I picked up their feet an' tied three feet and then I'd tie the hind foot up and let 'em up and put a halter and bridle on 'em; let 'em up and handle 'em a little, and tie 'em to another mule. Caught the first one and put a harness on 'im, tied him to a gentle mule and turned him loose in the corral, an' then I caught the other'n the same way. I tied their heads together an' put a rope around them, tied it to the outside of the head and put it right around the hips. Then I put them together so they wouldn't turn out. After quite a little while, four or five days, I drove them with the mules; out on the grade haulin' dirt. Then to haul rock there was five teams, ten mules. I steered with a jerk line. The jerk line run up to the dent on the nine mule and they had their heads together, tied in a line which run across and you would pull on that, pull 'em to the left and jerk 'em and holler, "Geeee," and turn 'em to the right. One way was a steady pull and the other way was a jerk.

Pa could gentle any animal, but horses were his first love and he could train them to do most anything.

It was a bad year for cattle. The winters of 1886 and 1887 were the worst on record in those parts; most cattleman lost everything they had, lock, stock and barrel. That winter was called "The Great Die-up," on the Northern Plains and it left nearly every rancher scratchin' gravel. At the beginning of 1886 cattlemen had two million cattle valued at sixty million dollars. By spring of 1887 they had lost a million animals and forty million dollars. One cattleman woke up to find he'd lost six hundred head in one single night!

Pa's job breakin' mules was over as soon as the Evans Hotel was built and he went to looking for something to do. It was so hard to find work, you had to wait for someone to die to get a job. The railroad was building up from the south and Pa packed water for the workmen. He remembered when Alliance, Nebraska contained only two tents, a saloon and a general store. Once he went to Rapid City, "and for two or three hours in the afternoon you wouldn't even see a dog cross the street." He had his best times in Rapid when cowboys staged rodeos right on Main Street. One day, he roped a steer on the sidewalk in front of where Flynn's Bookstore was later located. "Whenever we got together in Rapid it always seemed to rain," Pa said. "I started seventeen horses down Main Street past the Harney Hotel. I couldn't see 'em for the mud and water." Another time half the town was bettin' on whether Sam Bunker, a stubborn Englishman, could ride a horse named Black Andy. I told him not to whip or spur the horse cause I'd raised him. Bunker paid no attention, scratched him with a spur, cracked him with a quirt—and was thrown under the high boardwalk right in front of the First National Bank. The horse ran into the open door of a blacksmith shop where Pa caught and soothed him. Pa sold Black Andy to Russ Madison and Russ sold him to Buffalo Bill Cody.

Rapid City was Pa's favorite metropolis for all his adult years. He preferred the range, but Rapid had always drawn him. When he first saw it, there were only two blocks of buildings. Besides the rodeos there were horse races and stock meetings where Pa was often "Marshal of the Day," regulating all contests, including the races, ropin', and ridin':

> We use to buck wild horses for crowds on the sidewalks just for the hell of it. Drunken cowboys sometimes drove steers into the crowds and tried to rope 'em but they were too drunk. Sure had some big drinkin' bouts in those days. There was lots of shootin'. One time a cowboy named Borland refused to get rid of his gun in a saloon when the town marshal told him to. The marshal tried to take it away from him, Borland started shootin' and got himself hit in both sides. He kept comin', shootin' away, until the marshal dropped. They never arrested or bothered the cowboy in any way.

Townspeople knew when cowboys were likely to get paid, it was time to stay off the streets. When cowboys came galloping into town shootin' at windows, everybody cleared out. A few days of excitement in the city always sent Pa back to the range and the horses he loved:

> Folks just couldn't realize how good it was then or what might

*come," he always said. "A fella could take up a claim, earn a few
dollars and start with a few cows. He didn't have to own the land or
pay taxes. All it took was a little ambition and a lot of work. I had
1,500 horses when you didn't have to own a foot of land. One day
on the range with the help of three other fellas, I rode out ninety-six
wild horses, about nineteen a piece.*

In Pa's great old world of early manhood there was "nothin" but coyotes, gray wolves, horses, and cattle. He preferred such a world but had no greater liking for the wolves than he had for the cluttered society he survived to see. One winter he killed a wolf that weighed over one hundred and ten pounds but he lost more than one hundred colts to wolves that were capable of hamstringing a colt or a grown cow with one slash of fangs. A badly tossed lariat was snapped in two by razor sharp teeth. The wolf started to disappear when the bounty on the animal was raised to fifty dollars and professional hunters moved in.

Still workin' odd jobs in the spring of 1890, Pa wandered into Grandma Davis' yard near Rapid City. Her husband, Plummer C. Davis, had asthma, which nowadays might have been diagnosed as emphysema and he wandered around the country looking for a place he could breathe. Grace Josephine Davis, then a sweet little nine year old girl, was playing in the yard with her two brothers. Pa was hungry and he offered to split wood in exchange for a meal if they'd have him. He was still working for Grandma six months later putting in a garden. The children idolized him, especially Mama, the pretty, curly-top, who followed him around while he was doing chores. The highpoint of the day came when the kids talked him into plowing them under as he drove the horse and plow around the field. Mama soon found that nothing could put stars in her eyes like being buried alive in a mound of dirt! Grandma liked him too, because she said, "He kept a good woodpile."

Pa was helping out the Davis family and working for Hank Gould on the L. I. Horse Ranch when word came that South Dakota would become the fortieth state in the union! Wyoming, Washington, Montana, Idaho, and North Dakota all joined the union between 1888 and 1889, with much rejoicing and carryin' on in the streets, bands playin' "Yankee Doodle Dandy," church bells ringing, and parades galore. About that same time the Great Sioux Reservation was broken up when the Indians signed the 1889 land cession, giving up nine million acres of land that would soon be opened for settlement. At admission to statehood South Dakota land was valued at about one hundred million dollars and most of that ended up in the pockets of tough, ambitious ranchers, men who had fought their way to power and aimed to keep it that way. Folks said it took the cattlemen years to regain their losses from the "Die up," and then they came back with so much money they could have cleaned up the national debt and had enough left over for toothpicks!

Even though the summers of 1889 and 1890 were scorchers and farmers suffered the worst crops in years, people were still setting their sights on homesteadin' with dreams as big as Christmas hams. And no wonder; there weren't too many places in the world where a man could have a hundred and sixty acres just for the provin'. Foreigners from Ireland, Italy, and Russia poured into the United States, in fact, there were more Italians in New York City than there were in Italy! Politicians and merchants in Pierre, Sioux Falls, and Rapid City were fairly rubbing their greedy palms together hoping all those immigrants would end up in South Dakota.

RUSTLIN'

Arthur C. Mellette was voted first state Governor in 1889 and times were lookin' better. Homesteaders flocked into Rapid City hunting for land, while the old-time cowboys knew it spelled the end of the big ranches spreading over two states and beyond. Some ranchers didn't like it one little bit but there was nothing to do but accept their new neighbors and move over to make room. Pa said he could, "ride the entire length of the new state without runnin' up against a single barbed wire fence and a horse could run one hundred and eighty miles," free as a crow flies.

Pa went to breakin' horses for the Allied Horse Ranch, again for the unheard of salary of fifty dollars a month, utilizing his amazing bronc-bustin' skills. Since ranches depended on good mounts, a man with Pa's ability wasn't just considered a puncher, he was a "top" hand, he knew horses better than people, knew how to care for them, keep them in good shape, and get the maximum work out of them. Pa often said he'd never seen a horse he couldn't ride. "Once you get a rope on 'em, you can gentle all of 'em. I can get on 'em within five minutes after the rope's on." But Pa encountered many wild horses in the Badlands he couldn't catch. These he shot and sent to packing plants: "I used to like to get hold of these outlaws and hitch 'em up." He told of a time when he and Charles Hubbel roped a couple of wild geldings, tied them up and put harnesses on them. They tied their heads and tails together and hitched them to a heavy spring wagon, made from an old stagecoach. Hubbel and Pa drove into Rapid City, pulled up at Alex Shellito's livery barn and told Shellito to "unhitch 'em." Of course, Pa had to take care of them after a few minutes, but he had his fun scarin' hell out of Shellito.

There was as much difference in horses as there was in cowpunchers, even though one horse looked pretty much like another to a stranger. Every horse was an individual; some were "churn-heads," "cutting horses," "carving," "peg-ponies" or "saddlers." One of the best horses was a rope horse, sure-footed, and clear-sighted. If a horse was mean, a "snake blood," it was generally because some fool bronc-peeler had misused him.

Pa ran horses from the Little Missouri to the Nebraska line. He (usually) branded colts he found belonging to other horse ranchers with the same brand

Dinner on the trail.

their mother had. Other owners did the same for Pa when they ran across his colts. In those days the Cheyenne and Belle Fourche Rivers were filled to their banks. Pa often had to swim his horses:

> *There's nothin' to it. Jes' tap 'em lightly on the head to get 'em to go the way you want 'em to. When an old mare would lose track of her colt while swimmin' she would mill around in the middle — swim in a circle — and the others would follow behind her. Then I'd have to break it up and get 'em headed to the other side. Not all horses are good swimmers. When I got one like that, I'd slide off and hold onto its tail or else hold the saddle horn and swim beside it.*

Come November 1890, most cowboys from the Allied, VVV, and Circle Bar had some time off and Pa used these vacations galloping for the army as a scout. Some of that scouting involved gettin' a little fresh meat for the army camps. Pa "borrowed" steers from big cattle drives going back South or coming up to summer pasture in the North, as the case might be. I suspect some of those borrowed critters found their way into pastures other than the army stew pots and no doubt contributed to some of the large herds that later developed. The army depended on real cowboys to procure beef (one way or the other) for the camps and if blame went to the Indians, well, that was even better. If a fella wasn't too bright, he got caught, like the time Gene Aiken, Richard Meiners, James Girton, and Lewis Everly caught Frank Diamond and Charley Curly getting careless with their brandin' irons near Hermosa. There was no neck-tie social for these two long riders, just a couple of shots brought em' down dead as door nails. The vigilantes were later tried for manslaughter and found innocent as new-born babes.

Another story Pa always told was about the time Francis Rush was accused of horse stealing and the boys who chased him down were about ready to string him up to the nearest tree for a little strangulation jig. He told them if they'd let him go, he'd stay out of the country and never steal another horse. His judge and jury of several men were just as glad to excuse him, as no one really wanted to hang an erstwhile buddy who had saved their scalps a number of times! This man Rush went to Rapid City, got into the hauling business, started a Transfer Company, and never rustled another horse, or so they say. Nowadays, we call that successful vocational rehabilitation.

Cattle rustlin' was an established business in the Dakotas. Most cowboys were idle during the winter months and with a good horse or two they began "mavericking." When a calf left its mother without a brand they were considered maverick waifs on the range. In the Badlands, the wilder the country the more mavericks there were to be found. If a cowpoke ran onto mavericks in valleys sheltered by trees or rocks, it was easy to "cut" them out, brand them or possibly slit the tongue so the calf couldn't suckle and would leave its mother. After

Log house on the Circle Bar Ranch.

the "Great Die-up," many a rustler was in evidence, in fact the country was crawlin' with them. The whitest knights on the range started out "learnin' the ropes" as the blackest sheep.

Horse stealing often resulted in a necktie party. To steal a man's horse left him afoot in dangerous country, no sin was greater in the eyes of the western rancher. Pa only had one occasion to be troubled by a horse thief. He counted his horses one morning and there were quite a few missing. He trailed them for several days, gettin' madder and madder as time went on. He finally found his horses pastured east of Fairburn along French Creek and took them home. The man who stole them was never seen again. Folks said he must have left the area for good, one way or another.

STIRRIN' UP THE GHOST DANCERS

When the terrifying rumors of the "Ghost Dance" reached Rapid City, Grandma Davis was mighty glad to see Pa come around to make sure everybody was all right. Up and down the Cheyenne River and as far north as North Dakota all the way down to Nebraska, settlers brought their families into the nearest towns in case of an Indian uprising. By November of 1890, the streets of Rapid City were full of people afraid to go back to their ranches. It looked bad. Of the twenty-six thousand Sioux estimated in 1890, at least ten thousand lived on the Pine Ridge and Rosebud Reservations, less than a hundred miles away and that was too close for comfort. An article in the December 19, 1890 Hermosa Pilot tells how the settlers were protecting themselves:

If there ever existed a state of affairs that exasperated American citizens with this Government beyond all moderate expression, it is the manner in which the military authorities have neglected protecting the lives and property of the residents of the eastern portion of Custer county, along the borders of the reservation. For weeks. . .these blood-thirsty red-skins have succeeded in frightening people from their homes, causing them great hardship and expense that they are wholly unable to bear. And this, when we daily read of so many hundred soldiers lingering idly about the agency, and other points of quiet retreat, where the ugly warring savage is least likely to go. These troops have been seriously needed along the Cheyenne River, . . .for the past few weeks, and they were called for but came not, until last week. Ye Gods! Isn't it enough to boil the blood of a lover of home and country?. . . Last week the magnanimous military authorities ordered about 100 soldiers. . .while thousands of the blue coated gentry were merrily engaged killing time, safely away from where the horny handed citizens were driven to the desperate and painful past-time of killing Indians.

Pa in the Home Guard—1890.

Rumors were flying around like leaves in a high wind. All the redskins had broken loose! They're just over the river! The agents have lost all control! A man was reported killed and scalped and all his friends were sad for a week until one day up the street he walks as bright as a penny. Pa was riding along the Cheyenne River from the mouth of Spring Creek when he heard a rumor that "Three of Stenger's men got killed by Indians over by the cow camps. Old Two-Sticks was

20

one of them and they came in there at night, and the cowboys got supper for 'em and they went away. The men went to bed and that night the damned Indians come back and killed 'em with their own axe when they was asleep." That story sure riled everybody up!

With Pa's reputation for handlin' a horse, he and some other boys were picked by Col. M.H. Day to help out the cowboy militia they called the Home Guard. After all the rumors, ranchers were just waitin' for Indians to cross the Cheyenne River and head for Rapid City after raiding the settlements in between. Even before they formed the Home Guard, ranchers petitioned Governor Arthur C. Mellette for arms and ammunition. The Governor sent his old friend Col. Merritt H. Day hundreds of guns and plenty of ammunition so the cowboys were well armed and ready for a little fun. Col. Day came up with the idea to use the younger boys to stir up the Indians by rushing into their Ghost Dances, shootin' em up and then hightailing it back to where Day and the older men were waiting in ambush. Pa remembered one of the most exciting days of his life:

There was a bunch of men there. We went over and stirred them (Indians) up and a lot of our fellows laid in at the head of a gulch. We kids went over to the Stronghold and got 'em after us and they chased us down Corral Draw. Riley Miller was at the head of it and layin' up there behind the trees and rocks. This Riley Miller was a dead shot, and he just killed them Indians as fast as he could shoot. Francis Roush, Roy Coates, George Cosgrove, Paul McClellan was with us. We killed about seventy-five of them. Riley Miller and Frank Lockhart went back there and got some pack horses and brought out seven loads of guns, shirts, war bonnets, ghost shirts and things. Riley took 'em to Chicago and started a museum. He made a barrel of money out of it.

Pa had quite a few adventures during those wild and wooly Home Guard days:

We was ridin' all the time, everyday. We were out lookin' for Indians across the river, seein' if there wasn't a bunch comin' around there. One night I was there with Riley Miller, and M.H. Day. There was about ten of us, Francis Roush, George Cosgrove, Paul McClellan and Frank Hart and the rest of 'em. We got dinner, and had a guard out, and George Cosgrove was the oldest fellow in the bunch. He was gonna take care of us and stand guard. We just got dinner ready and were ready to eat biscuits and bacon, 'bout all we had to eat, and the guard come in and said there was a bunch of horsemen comin' up the river. He didn't know if they were Indians or what they were. Cosgrove got out his field glasses and said "They are Indians and there are seventeen of 'em. You fellows get behind everything you can see, so they can't hit ya, and don't shoot until I holler at ya." The house was settin' on the flat there and the corral was right east of it and our horses were in there saddled, and these Indians come up over the bank right out of the river onto the flat, and it wasn't over seventy yards from the house and when they come up over the hill there, I was right out in front of the house, behind the wood pile and I never waited for Cosgrove to holler or nothin'. I just went to shootin' and by gawd, we knocked off five of 'em and them Indians jumped off and went to pickin' 'em up and put 'em across the front of another saddle and away they went. Francis Roush was there and I was not over fifteen to twenty feet from him behind this woodpile, and he was eatin'. Just went to eatin'. So, he picked up a biscuit and some bacon and come to the door and he had his rifle and he stood right in that door with his rifle. He would take a bite of biscuit and take a shot right in front of 'em.

Another time a man named Frank Hart and Pa went across the Cheyenne to "borrow" another beef. They saw soldiers camped nearby:

They was camped up on Finney Flats with some wagons, mules and things and we saw 'em as we came back. I roped a big, fat steer and started back across the river with him. It was frozen over and slick and I had a sharp-shod horse. The Indians were up three or four hundred yards from us. Frank had a lisp when he talked and I says to Frank, I says, "git around this steer. Let's git him across this river and git the hell outa here!" "Oh, he says," "They can't hit uth, they're way up there in them thedars." Well they were plenty close enough and so I run this steer on down to the river and Frank right along side of 'em. I went ahead of him and I jerked the steer on to the ice, and slid him across the river and there was five bullets hit the ice right as we was goin' across. Frank kept sayin' "Oh they can't hit uth." We got out of there and went up the draw and got away from 'em. The soldiers had a fence, a saddle horse pasture. The soldiers were camped there inside of that. I went to put this damned steer through the gate and he jumped over the fence. I let Frank take the rope and he got on the inside of the fence and took the rope and headed him right into the wagon! This big damned steer run up and there was a lot of soldiers standin' there and Frank was headin' that steer right into 'em. The soldiers got up on the wagon and he got the steer outa there and they was a-yellin' and a-cussin' him. Frank went to laughin' so we got that steer and killed him for beef. Some of those soldiers saw the Indians and they went down and killed six of 'em. We heard the shootin' but we didn't know what happened until the next day when (Joe) McCloud and them fellows came down wearing those Indian's clothes. They had their guns, brought 'em right on down where we were on the edge of the Finney Flats.

At Cole Ranch near the mouth of Spring Creek (right about where the railroad bridge is located) Pa had another run-in with Ghost Dancers:

There was three Indians come in there and Warren Cole was standing guard in the barn with a shotgun, loaded with buckshot, and one of these Indians went to the door, and just as he showed up, Warren shot him with the shotgun. Killed him dead. Then they (the Home Guard) was afraid the Indians would come back there that night or the next day so they sent down for ten soldiers from Col. Carr's command to come up and help 'em stand guard. Well, Paul McClelland and Frank Hart and I rode in there that night and we'd been over ridin' across the river, around Sheep Mountain to see if we could see any Indians and we come in there and helped them to stand guard. I and Paul went down the river and I don't know where Frank was standin', around there somewhere. These soldiers in the stack yard; they put their horses in the stack yard, between the stacks; these nigger soldiers made their beds in there between the stacks. By God, they was sleepin' out there and one of them niggers heard a sound and he got so scared he raised up and shot his own horse!

The settlers had check points or "forts" at certain locations along the river in case Indians came around, they'd be waitin' for them. The rule was, when any suspicious sounds or gunshots were heard, everyone was to drop flat on the floor and let the scouts handle it. One night someone shot an Indian across the river and among the group in one of those "forts" was a very gentlemanly, distinguished, and highly proper man named Keliher who happened to be in the vicinity when news of the little disturbance forced him to take shelter. During the night, the horses raised a ruckus and everyone dropped to the floor in the darkness. The only sound was the beating of hearts. After what seemed hours, an old Irish woman, Mrs. McCabe, who did the washing for the men yelled out, "Keliher, let go me laig!" The great guffaw that followed her outburst of Irish humor must have scared off the rest of the Indians!

The boys were scoutin' one afternoon when they met up with Gus Craven:

He come down off the hill there from the table down on Spring Creek. About where Joe Reed lived later on, where that hill is comin' off of Finney Flats. And man! Was he ridin'! When he was

23

The Badlands.

comin' down close to the river on the other side, a couple of Indians come out and took after him. He got away as fast as he could and his horse pulled back and broke the rope. He was leading his own horse and ridin' the big government one. And we met him down at the foot of the hill and he was a comin' and then the Indians come down over that hill aways and they saw us and they turned and went back. And old Gus, he was sure a scared boy! He couldn't get his gun out of the holster and his horse was pullin' back and he broke the rope and got away but I'll tell you he was scared. "God," he says, "I'm glad to meet you fellas!" We didn't catch those Indians. We looked for them all afternoon and never could find them . . .They just disappeared in the Badlands. We rode all over Sheep Mountain and around that country, Paul McClellan, Frank and I.

Pa and the cowboys stirred up the Indians quite a few times that fall of 1890, in fact, they never left them alone, but he especially remembered getting caught out by himself one day on the south side of the river while he was huntin' Indians. He hunkered down in a ditch behind some sage brush most all day waiting for three figures he'd seen on a ridge to go away. Come to find out, it was only three trees on the horizon, but three against one, he didn't dare take the chance!

Pa's days in the Home Guard came to a temporary halt on December 20, 1890. An excerpt from the Dec. 21, Rapid City Journal relates the story:

Last night two messengers came in from the Plummer C. Davis ranch on Spring Creek in search of a physician to attend a young man named Peter Lemley who had accidently shot himself with a Winchester rifle. From the men who came in, it was learned Lemley had been tinkering with a gun when it accidently discharged, the ball striking his right side and passing out his back. The young man is dangerously hurt and from what information that could be gathered from the men who came to town for the doctor, is not expected to live. Lemley is about twenty-one years of age and is spoken of by those who know him as a most exemplary man.

Pa's version was a little different:

Well, I was settin' in the chair sewing up the holster. It was a Colt 45. The holster had ripped when I was fightin' Indians. I stuck the gun in to see how it was goin' to fit and I loosened up on the holster and the gun fell out and the hammer hit on the chair, on the edge of the chair right close to me. Not much powder burn, had my shirt on. I wasn't knocked out, but I just stayed there and held my shirt to it and let the blood run out on the floor. I was at Davis' on Spring Creek. I had a doctor, an old doctor who lived out there on the divide. The doctor said the bullet went in on the right, and hit my right lung. Coughed up blood. I was down with that about three weeks. I didn't ride right away, but was ridin' in less than a month. They didn't have penicillin in those days and the doctor wanted to probe for the bullet, but I told him I was hurtin' bad enuf. I didn't want no damn probin' for a bullet!

Pa knew if he'd let that doctor carve him up, he'd been a goner. Sixty years later when he had a chest x-ray, doctors found the bullet lodged in his heart muscle. Pa was shot near the heart and lived! Maybe that's why he was so damned hardhearted.

Pine Ridge — 1890.

THE WOUNDED KNEE MASSACRE

Sitting Bull was killed along about December 15, 1890, and if folks weren't scared enough as it was, they were certain after the medicine man was done in, that all hell was goin' to break loose. Buffalo Bill was sent out to try and talk to Sitting Bull but Major James McLaughlin, Agent at Standing Rock, got Cody drunk as a skunk and had his orders changed before Bill knew what had happened to him. Cody never could hold his liquor and it was easy enough to waylay him. McLaughlin wanted the glory of catching Sitting Bull himself and he wasn't goin' to let Buffalo Bill show him up. The wily agent gave his Indian police orders to arrest Sitting Bull and "not let him escape under any circumstances," so they didn't let him escape. At the crack of dawn the police closed in on the chief but the old warrior decided he didn't like the looks of things. Lone Man, an Indian witness, later recalled that "It was like trying to extinguish a treacherous prairie fire." Sitting Bull's followers went wild, shook their fists, and cursed the policemen, "You will not take our chief!" A terrible fight broke out which left Sitting Bull, his young son, and six policemen dead; they had all gotten a little too close to the griddle. News of the killings spread like wildfire across the state and nation but for the people in the settlements close to the Pine Ridge Reservation, it was like settin' right on top of a beehive.

Buffalo Bill said later he never had the slightest intention of arresting Sitting Bull as they had been personal friends for years. The chief was still ridin' a beautiful trained showhorse Cody had given him after touring with Buffalo Bill in 1885. Pa said that when the Indian police went to arrest Sitting Bull, that old show horse heard the shootin' and automatically went into his Wild West routine, stood up and walked on his hind legs right there in the corral next to the cabin. But Agent McLaughlin was jealous of Cody's friendship with the chief and was tryin' to show that Sitting Bull was a Ghost Dance leader, which subsequent events proved false.

McLaughlin had reason to be jealous of Buffalo Bill Cody. Beginning in the last quarter of the nineteenth century western mania took ahold of the hearts and minds of Americans. One man stepped into the center of that magical stage and the world was never the same again. William F. Cody, Buffalo Bill, organized what he called the "Wild West Show," in 1883. He started in Nebraska and before he died in 1917, his name was a household word in every part of the world. America never had such a beloved, goodwill ambassador, the ever optimistic, dashing, hard-drinkin' man who earned and lost more fortunes in his lifetime than five millionaires rolled into one. His indomitable spirit, and charismatic genius brought together the best Indian horsemen, western cowboys, and cowgirls the world had ever seen. They carried western glamor to a world that had only read about the frontier and wanted to share in all the excitement.

The mere mention of Buffalo Bill brought a twinkle to the eye of every lad in the country. Wherever he appeared, crowds of youngsters followed him, waiting to shake the hand or hear a word from the greatest western showman in American history. And he never let them down.

William F. Cody was ten years old when his father died and he went right to work as a herder mounted on a small mule. In time, he advanced to a wagonmaster and at fourteen made a name for himself as a Pony Express Rider. He joined the Seventh Kansas Cavalry as a scout, Indian fighter, and plainsman, and later earned his name supplying buffalo meat for the Kansas Pacific Railroad crew with a needle-gun, a breech-loading 50-caliber Springfield rifle he called "Lucretia Borgia." Cody rode as a scout on buffalo hunts with the Grand Duke Alexis of Russia and got into many a fight with Indians along the way. For his exceptional bravery under fire with the Seventh Cavalry, not unlike Indian warriors who earned eagle feathers for bravery, Cody won the Congressional Medal of Honor and he proudly possessed the medal for the remaining forty-four years of his life.

Cody didn't hate Indians, in fact, he respected their superb horsemanship and fearless bravery. As long as they treated him fairly, and did right by him, he was a friend to the Indians and could speak several Indian dialects. The feeling was mutual and Cody counted among his friends, Sitting Bull, the famous warchief Red Cloud, Rain-In-The-Face, American Horse, Gall, Crow Dog, and many others, all of whom galloped beside him all around the world in the Wild West Shows. Buffalo Bill Cody might have stopped the violence which ended with the Wounded Knee Massacre on December 29, 1890, stopped it with straight talk and friendship, if it hadn't been for the jealous interference of Major James McLaughlin.

Meanwhile, General Nelson A. Miles was tryin' to orchestrate the whole Indian campaign from his headquarters in Chicago, but when he heard about the ruckus on the Cheyenne and the death of Sitting Bull, he moved his plush headquarters in Chicago to an equally plush suite of rooms at the Harney Hotel in Rapid City. The whole town knew he was sittin' up there on his duff when he should have been in the field. He gave Home Guard Commander Col. Merritt H. Day orders not to cross the Cheyenne but of course Col. Day just ignored him and went anyway. The Home Guard boys knew the territory like the back of their hands and were havin' too much fun raisin' hell to let a little military pomp stand in their way.

By December 20, 1890, Rapid City was fairly crawlin' with soldiers, which was good for the freightin' outfits, saloons, and storekeepers. Tom Sweeney owned the hardware store and he was doin' a landslide business along with all the local hotels and merchants.

Pa was recuperatin' at the Davis ranch, lettin' Mama wait on him hand and foot. She thought he was a real hero for sure and Grandma Davis was glad to have him there in case the Indians attacked. But he wasn't happy at all to be out of the saddle. In fact, they nearly had to tie him down when he heard the Home Guard was stirring up the Indians again. What a time to go and shoot yourself! Pa fumed and Grandma made him lie down. No tellin' what would have happened to him if he hadn't listened to reason. Mama read to Pa in the evenings and he just lay there staring at the ceiling, muttering to himself, wishing he was with the boys on the Cheyenne. It was there on the quiet moonlit nights when Pa was flat on his back, that my innocent Mother fell madly in love with the gallant protector she imagined Pa to be.

On December 30, 1890, came the news of the Wounded Knee Massacre of the day before. The Seventh Cavalry under Col. James W. Forsyth, had surrounded Chief Big Foot and his band near Porcupine Butte. While trying to disarm the Indians at Wounded Knee Creek, a fight broke out leaving one hundred fifty-three Indian men, women and children dead on the battlefield, and forty-four wounded. Countless others ran wounded from the scene or were picked up by their own people during the blizzard following the tragedy. White casualties included one officer killed, six noncommissioned officers, and eighteen privates. Thirty-nine others were wounded and some died afterward. Bodies were found three miles from the scene, meaning that some soldiers carried things too far. Officers were said to have been drinking and boastin' the night before, which might have caused problems that bloody morning. The newspapers had been taunting the Seventh Cavalry to avenge Custer, accusing them of being afraid. Many of the soldiers in the Seventh weren't even American citizens, had only been in service two weeks, couldn't read or write, let alone speak English or follow orders in a language foreign to their own. Those were the kind of men that should never have been there anyway, and later they made the whole episode look bad for the rest of the men who weren't expecting any trouble and got caught right in the middle of it, many of them falling from bullets fired from their own men in a crossfire.

News of dead soldiers made Pa's blood boil! He wanted his horse. Where's his saddle? Get him outta this bed, he was goin' to help the boys! Pa got into the saddle alright, but Mother Nature interrupted to give him a few more days of unwanted rest. A blizzard rushed in with temperatures forty degrees below zero and howling winds that shook the porch railings and clattered shed doors open and shut. Nobody went anywhere until January 1, 1890, when a military burial detail from Pine Ridge went out to bury the dead on Wounded Knee Creek.

Pa rode over to Wounded Knee to see what had happened and it wasn't an easy ride. Lakota warriors were everywhere and Pa had to be mighty careful to sneak by them to reach Wounded Knee. Although he made that ride alone in freezing weather, hurt as he was with a bullet in his chest, he never mentioned it once. All he said about the massacre was what he heard from others:

> *Big Foot was sick and the soldiers held him up there and he surrendered the night before the battle. The next morning Col. Forsyth lined up two rows of soldiers, left about thirty feet between them. They marched those Indians up and they was to leave their guns there after they got through the line of soldiers. There was a medicine man there and he reached down and picked up a handful of dust and throwed it up and after that they all began shootin' at one another. The soldiers couldn't shoot until they formed a line and got out of there, they couldn't shoot cause they would have shot each other. The Indians did quite a little damage; killed twenty-five soldiers. Them Indians was a-runnin'...but a (German) fella with a hotchkiss gun (Cpl. Paul H. Weinert) killed most of the Indians. His partner got shot off the gun, (Lt. Harry L. Hawthorne) and also got his own little finger shot off. It made him mad, and he just went to shootin' every Indian he could see. The last one was an old man goin' up the draw with a covered wagon, and he had it full of women and babies. There was just some little Indian babies lived through it.*

Pa always thought Big Foot had made it out alive too but the old chief was one of the first to die right out in front of his own tent. Later photographs of the battlefield show Big Foot's corpse, half sittin' up with a frozen look of bewilderment on his face.

Pa got to Wounded Knee as "they was gettin' some of the soldiers out; loadin' 'em up in ambulances or anything that would travel. They got the Indians buried, most of 'em right there at the battlefield." Buffalo Bill came over to Wounded Knee with General Miles the same day Pa got there. Of course, the General was about a month too late but he stomped around givin' orders, huffin' and puffin' like he was going to jump in and save the world. Folks said that was his usual way of doin' things—to wait until everything looked hopeless and then come along and clean it up and get all the credit!

Bill Cody noticed a slender young man, as fast as a fox and as agile on a horse as any man he'd ever seen. He called him over and Buffalo Bill Cody and Pete Lemley struck up a friendship that day at Wounded Knee that was to last many years. The only good thing that ever came out of the Indian scare was his new friendship with the showman he called, "a real guy." Even though Pa was carryin' a Colt slug in his chest, his expert ridin' ability so impressed Buffalo Bill that he asked Pa to join him that coming spring for a tour of Europe with his Wild West Show! He was takin' some of the Ghost Dance leaders with him to ease the tension at Pine Ridge, including Kicking Bear and Short Bull, and he wanted Pete Lemley to go with him. Most men would have jumped at the chance, but Pa was no hyprocrite. He didn't know if he wanted to eat and sleep alongside Indians he'd been shootin' at two weeks before. Besides, he'd already promised Col. Day that he'd work for him at spring round-up. No, thanks anyway Bill, he didn't think he could go, but he suggested Cody take Russ Madison, a fella he called, "the fastest, quickest cowboy you ever saw." Madison became one of Cody's best performers that season when they toured Europe. Buffalo Bill didn't forget the "Badlands Fox" he met at Wounded Knee as future events proved, but Pa wasn't ready for the "Greatest Western Show On Earth" just yet. His time would come anyway, and he knew he had been one of the last Indian fighters of the old frontier, and he was proud of it. There would never be any others like them in the history of the west.

WITH BUFFALO BILL'S WILD WEST

In 1893, Buffalo Bill suggested to Russ Madison that he round up some good broncos from South Dakota and while he was at it, grab that son-of-a-gun cowboy, Pete Lemley, the one who refused to join his European tour in '91.' Cody wanted the best cowboys for a season with the Wild West Show and Congress of Rough Riders of the World at the World's Columbian Exposition in Chicago.

Russ talked Pa into tryin' it, but he didn't like the idea of being around so many people for any longer than he had to. A whole new age had dawned in America, history called it the "Gilded Age." Pa recuperated from the bullet wound in his chest and he was just young enough to enjoy all that life in the "Gay 90s" had to offer.

Many South Dakota Indians and cowboys who took part in the Wild West Show outfitted in Rushville, Nebraska and took the train from Rushville in special cars. Cody paid for all the trimmings, for the tickets, and even the food. Some took their own horses but the show provided beautiful mounts shipped in from all over the United States. Arrangements snagged for a time in Chicago when the World's Fair officials informed Buffalo Bill and his handsome partner, Nate Salsbury, that there wasn't enough room for their show on the Exposition grounds. But Salsbury was too fast for them. He leased fourteen acres between 62nd Street and 63rd Street, right across from the entrance to the Columbian Exposition! The grandstand seated 18,000 cheering fans, with room for the Indian camp and tents for the cowboys and other performers.

On May 1, 1893, the Exposition opened when President Grover Cleveland pressed a new-fangled electric key in a plush purple box, which was supposed to start all the electric machinery at the fair. He gave a speech saying everything was stupendous... magnificent... proud destiny... brotherhood... and a lot of other high falutin' words politicians love to hear themselves say. Hundreds of bright colored flags were hoisted up and at the same moment warships on the lake shot off their loud guns, four trained lions roared, the crowds screamed, ladies fainted and cried out, ambulances and stretcher-bearers carried off the injured, and Pa wished he'd stayed home.

With Buffalo Bill's Wild West 1895-96 (?) — left to right —
Bottom row center—Russ Madison

It was a good thing Cody put his people up in tents because Pa soon found out that hotels, even the Cattleman's Hotel on 16th Street cost a whoppin' dollar a day, which was big money to a range cowboy's pocket. There was so much to see at the fair—people just walked around with their mouths open until their feet hurt so bad they had to sit down and take their shoes off to see if they still had feet. The Exposition was right on the lakefront, a grandiose plaster-of-paris "White City" full of Greek temples, reflecting pools, and big statues of nude men and women! On the Midway a fella could pay fifty cents to see a two hundred pound woman dressed in girdles and skirt, kick up her legs in a hootchy-kootchy dance. The overweight belly dancer was a middle eastern floozy named "Little Egypt" and she stole the show. A newspaper described her act:

Waving two scarlet handkerchiefs of silk, she moves slowly around, her arms gleaming through her sleeves of gauze. Now she revolves and turns, her face assuming a dreamy smile, her painted eyes half closed, her white teeth showing between lips made redder and fuller by art. Now she begins the contortions that mark all the Oriental dances; her movements are snake-like and wanton, and she sinks lower and lower, wriggling, twisting, jerking, her face half veiled with her handkerchief, until she almost touches the stage, after the fashion which startled even Paris herself not so very long ago. At the close of the dance, the girl sits cross legged on the divan smoking cigarettes.

Besides the girly shows there was the first Ferris Wheel Pa or anyone else had ever seen. Sandow the Strongman, an Irish village, Castle Blarney, Ali Baba and the Forty Thieves, and Maude Adams starred in a production of Peter Pan. Pa got tired of the girly shows as soon as he and his money parted ways.

Owen Wister hadn't yet written "The Virginian," so Pa didn't know how strong and glamorous a cowboy he was. But he was soon to find out. The streets were crowded with people pushing this way and that, the food was expensive, and homeless waifs prowled the streets looking for handouts while they picked pockets. There had been a sudden panic on Wall Street that summer and a severe depression hit the United States, the symptoms of which weren't yet botherin' the crowds who were comin' to the fair in droves.

Major John Burke, Buffalo Bill's crafty publicity agent, had Pa and the boys put up posters all over Chicago:

AN ABSOLUTELY ORIGINAL AND HEROIC ENTERPRISE OF INIMITABLE LUSTRE . . . ITS GREAT ORIGINATOR NOW RIDES ALONG FAME'S WARPATH . . . A HOLIDAY REFLECTING YEARS OF ROMANCE AND THE REALITY OF IMPERISHABLE DEEDS, MAKING THE NEW WORLD AND THE OLD APPEAR IN BRAVEST AND MOST BRILLIANT RIVALRIES. THE CROWNED HEADS OF EUROPE WILL BE THERE. A YEAR'S VISIT WEST IN THREE HOURS!!

Chicago—1893 with Buffalo Bill's Wild West

Major Burke took full advantage of the recent Ghost Dance scare with painted posters exploiting the scenes where Buffalo Bill and General Miles made peace with the Indians. His Wild West Show opened a month before the Exposition with feature articles appearin' in all the newspapers. Reporters crowded around the cowboys and Indians for daily interviews and photographs. Pa wasn't too comfortable next to Chief Rain-In-The-face, who boasted he'd killed Tom Custer at the Battle of the Little Bighorn! Chief Standing Bear came in a warbonnet made of two hundred eagle feathers and said he was the richest Indian in America. Pa just couldn't believe it when he saw that Buffalo Bill had purchased Sitting Bull's bullet-splintered cabin, the one he was living in when he and his son were killed, and had the darn thing set up as part of the show. Chief Rocky Bear and American Horse seemed friendly enough, but Short Bull and Kicking Bear, the Ghost Dance leaders, were quiet and aloof and Pa stayed clear of them.

Annie Oakley's tent was a major attraction. Journalist Stewart H. Holbrook said of her:

She stood quite alone in her celebrity which cannot be likened to that of any currently famous female. Her flavor was unique and of her time. It was a sort of combination of Lillian Russell and Buffalo Bill, a merger of dainty feminine charm and lead bullets, the whole draped in gorgeous yellow buckskin and topped with a halo of powder-blue smoke.

The little sharp-shooter had planted flowers all around her tent and Amy Leslie, another writer went to visit her:

Her tent is a bower of comfort and taste. A bright Axminster carpet, cougar skins and buckskin trappings all about in artistic confusion — she had a glass of wine waiting and a warm welcome.

Pa noticed Annie was a sweet, docile woman, and she radiated that strong appeal to all the cowboys. There wasn't a one who wouldn't have died for her.

The cowboys lived in tents apart from the Indians but they all ate together in the mess tent where cooks made soup in great heavy iron kettles. The food was good, too, with fresh baked bread everyday and loads of griddlecakes and syrup.

Buffalo Bill was forty-seven years old and he cut a handsome figure on horseback. A magical aura surrounded him but he treated Pa and the other performers like an ordinary man. You could come up to him and he'd focus all his attention on you, made a fella feel like the most important man in the world. Sometimes he'd stop in the middle of a group of small boys and go down on one knee. They'd all cluster around him while he gave them advice that went something like this:

Now fellas, I want you to go to school and get an education. Don't play hooky, don't cuss, and be good to your mom. And most of all, be kind to animals.

The flamboyant mayor of Chicago, Carter Harrison, asked the Exposition officials to admit poor children free on a special day, but they refused. That really got Buffalo Bill hot! He sprang forward with the announcement that the Wild West Show would not only let them in free, but he'd also provide free transportation, free candy, and all the ice-cream they could eat! Fifteen thousand children, some so poor they just owned the clothes on their backs, came to see the show.

Major Burke set up a big publicity stunt, a seven hundred mile Cowboy Horse Race from Chadron, Nebraska to Chicago with considerable prize money for the winner. Pa knew he could beat them all with his hands tied, but he just sat back and watched while six or seven cowboys, among them the old-time bandit Doc Middleton, made fools out of themselves tryin' to win the race. They were pullin' all sorts of tricks on each other, takin' shortcuts, ridin' in wagons when they got tired, and even sending fresh mounts on ahead. In the end, Buffalo Bill couldn't decide who was the biggest cheater so he divided the prize money between them all!

The 1893 Wild West Show was the vintage year for Buffalo Bill. Six million paying customers saw his show, and with it the finest display of horsemanship ever seen. Besides President Cleveland, many famous people including Diamond Jim Brady, Susan B. Anthony, Princess Infanta of Spain, Lillian Russell, James Cardinal Gibbons, and nearly every notable journalist, artist, statesman, and scientist in America came to see Buffalo Bill and his Rough Riders.

Behind the scenes, it was a whole lot more interestin'. Seems Cody's wife was jealous of her husband's well-known lady friends. Cody spent, loaned, gave, and invested too much money when he was drunk, which was nearly all the time. Every Tom, Dick, and Harry wanted him to invest in some fool scheme or other and he usually did, but women were his weakness. A beautiful British actress, Katherine Clemmons, got Cody to spend $80,000 backing her productions and Mrs. Louisa Cody found out about it and came roaring into Bill's rented bungalow breaking furniture, cussin' up a storm, and cleaning house!

Usually, Bill Cody kept his private life separate from his show, except that everybody knew he sipped whiskey almost all day long. His marital problems spilled over into the show in Chicago when Mrs. Cody told several members of the troupe all about her womanizing husband. Pa and the other cowboys just looked down and kicked the dust when she walked by, but chuckled about it every time they saw her. Later on, Bill reportedly said of his affair with Miss Clemmons, "I'd rather manage a million Indians than one soubrette."

Pa was gettin' fed up with all the crowds, the dirty streets, the constant noise, side-show barkers hawking freak shows, and if it hadn't been for his friendship with Russ Madison, Pa would have left right off the bat. The 1893 World's Fair program was so popular that it remained the same for nearly a decade:

Buffalo Bill came galloping out, waving his cowboy hat in the air:
LADIES AND GENTLEMEN, PERMIT ME TO INTRODUCE TO
YOU A CONGRESS OF THE ROUGH RIDERS OF THE WORLD!
Overture, "Star Spangled Banner". . .Cowboy Band, William
Sweeny, Leader.
1. Grand Review introducing the Rough Riders of the World and
Fully Equipped Regular Soldiers of the Armies of America,
England, France, Germany, and Russia.
2. Miss Annie Oakley, Celebrated Shot, who will illustrate her
dexterity in the use of Fire-arms.
3. Horse race between a Cowboy, (sometimes Pa) a Cossack, a
Mexican, an Arab, and an Indian, on Spanish-Mexican, Broncho,
Russian, Indian, and Arabian Horses.
4. Pony Express. The Former Pony Post Rider will show how
the Letters and Telegrams of the Republic were distributed across
the immense Continent previous to the Railways and the Telegraph.
5. Illustrating a Prairie Emigrant Train Crossing the Plains.
Attack by "marauding" Indians repulsed by "Buffalo Bill" with Scouts
and Cowboys, (Pa included) The wagons are the same as used 35
years ago.
6. Group of Syrian and Arabian Horsemen will illustrate their
style of Horsemanship, with Native Sports and Pastimes.
7. Cossacks, of the Caucasus of Russia, in Feats of Horse-
manship, Native Dances, etc.
8. Johnny Baker, Celebrated Young American Marksman.
9. A Group of Mexicans from Old Mexico, will illustrate the use
of the Lasso, and perform various Feats of Horsemanship.
10. Racing Between Prairie, Spanish and Indian Girls.
11. Cowboy Fun. Picking Objects from the Ground, (a most
difficult and dangerous trick) Lassoing Wild Horses, (Pa, again)
Riding the Buckers.
12. Military Evolutions by a Company of the Sixth Cavalry of
the United States Army; a Company of the First Guard Uhlan
Regiment of His Majesty King William II, German Emperor,
popularly known as the "Potsdamer Reds"; a Company of French
Chasseurs (Chasseurs a Cheval de la Garde Republique Francais);
and a Company of the 12th Lancers (Prince of Wales' Regiment) of
the British Army.

13. *Capture of the Deadwood Mail Coach by the Indians, which will be rescued by "Buffalo Bill" and his attendant Cowboys. This is the identical old Deadwood Coach, called the Mail Coach, which is famous on account of having carried the great number of people who lost their lives on the road between Deadwood and Cheyenne 18 years ago. Now the most famed vehicle extant.*

14. *Racing Between Indian Boys on Bareback Horses.*

15. *Life Customs of the Indians. Indian Settlement on the Field and "Path."*

16. *Col. W. F. Cody ("Buffalo Bill"), in his Unique Feats of Sharpshooting.*

17. *Buffalo Hunt, as it is in the Far West of North America — "Buffalo Bill" and the Indians. The Last of the only known Native Herd.*

18. *The Battle of the Little Big Horn, Showing with Historical Accuracy the scene of Custer's Last Charge. (Early in the season the spectacle was: Attack on a Settler's Cabin — Capture by the Indians — Rescue by "Buffalo Bill" and the Cowboys.)*

19. *Salute. Conclusion.*

It was number eighteen on the program that got Pa a little excited. That was "art imitating life" if ever it could. It was hard to believe that Indians on hand to be obligingly run off were Kicking Bear, Short Bull, Plenty Horses, No Neck, Rocky Bear, Young-Man-Afraid-Of-His-Horses, and Jack Red Cloud, the son of Chief Red Cloud, the very same "blood-thirsty redskins" that Col. Day convinced the Home Guard to stir up and destroy.

Pa hated to walk anyplace, hated to be off his horse, and in Chicago a fella had to walk. The cowboys were spendin' their money hand over fist for flashy clothes, ladies of the evening, and all manner of trinkets Pa had absolutely no use for in the world. He always had to be on the alert to make sure his bedroll didn't get stolen! All the bad elements of the nation converged on Chicago hoping to lure unsuspecting cowboys to a friendly dishonest game of marked cards, or some high rollin' crap shooting, none of which interested Pa. The area was a field day for confidence men, fakers, harpies, thieves, and floozies of all kinds and colors. The saloons, dives of the filthiest kind, made a killing that summer in Chicago. There were hundreds of muggings, and robbings, and to top it all off, Mayor Harrison was assassinated right in his own doorway. God Forbid!

Pa liked Buffalo Bill, calling him, "A fella who could do anything, a western man through and through," but Pa had to get out while he still could. He'd had enough of the glamorous spotlight in the crowded, expensive city. It was the wide open range, the sound of birds in the morning, the smell of bacon on a campfire that called him back to good old South Dakota; clean air, pure water, and cow ponies. It never felt so good to be home.

Grandma Lucy F. Davis — She favored Pettigrew "because he kept a good woodpile."

THE MISSUS

After Pa came home from Buffalo Bill's Wild West, he went back to workin' for Col. Day at the Circle Bar Ranch on Lower Spring Creek. No matter where he went or how long he was gone, he always checked back with Grandma Davis to see if her woodpile was what it ought to be. At times, he must have noticed that Mama was growing up into a beautiful young woman with long, sun-flecked hair and eyes that lit up like twinkling stars whenever he came around, eyes that were attracted to Pa's strange, remote solitude, his mysterious side.

Mama was the pioneer daughter of Plummer C. Davis of Vermont, and the feisty Lucy Peabody, a relative of socially prominent George Peabody, financier and one of the foremost philanthropists of his time. Grandma Lucy was determined to leave snobbery behind her; the tight corsets, bunched-up bustles, and the layer upon layer of petticoats that made up "the refined lady." She was teaching school when she met the frail but handsome Plummer Davis, a man with his sights on Dakota Territory. She married the pioneer and they headed west. Lucy's tiny, four foot, eight inches belied the steel rod that went from the top of her head to the tips of her well-born toes. On the way to the Black Hills of South Dakota, Grandma Lucy gave birth to Grace Josephine, the fun-loving daughter of parents who believed women should be ladies, educated in the fine arts of the home, with the womanly ideals of self-sacrifice and religious instruction:

Dearest Gracie,
May you ever do the will of your Heavenly Father and follow
the teachings of the Savior who suffered and died for All is the
prayer of your,
Grandmother Peabody
December 27, 1887

The Davis family also wanted their daughter well educated with the possiblity of a career of her own. Mama was a jolly child, with a cheerful outlook

Grace Davis

on life, the heritage of a kindly mother and a generous father who doted on his only daughter. Their home was comfortable, full of lively children's squeals of laughter and pain, of cherished moments before the fire when Grandpa read the Bible aloud while Mama and her mother knitted, tatted, and sewed. Grandpa Davis also instilled in his daughter a firm religious faith. Occasionally, Mama found little reminders from her father in an ivory-covered autograph album, embossed with a masted sailing ship protected in stormy coastal waters by a beaming lighthouse of hope:

We spend our years as a tale that is told and let the beauty of the
Lord our God be upon us; teach us to number our days that we may
apply our hearts unto wisdom.
            Plummer C. Davis
            April 14, 1895

But it wasn't an easy religious life for man or woman on the frontier. A western woman's days were a constant round of cooking, baking, sewing, cleaning, ironing, mending, making fires, hauling water and wood, and numerous other tasks that were left for women to do. Lucy Peabody Davis was thrilled with the romance of the west, glad to leave behind forever the eastern society of her youth. Despite frontier hardships, she imparted a certain gentility to Mama, the unconscious product of graceful womanhood, the heredity and carriage of good breeding.

Some of Grandma's women neighbors were never meant to settle in the west, always complainin' about the harsh weather, the poor dugouts, the insects and snakes, and one thing and another. These women often left to return to city life in the east or lived out their lives of frustration and unhappiness, with either brutish husbands or weak-livered men who couldn't bring in a crop to save their good-for-nothing souls. These were the women with seven to ten children, whose hands were always red and parched, faces drawn, with backs bent from years of scrubbing. They died young and were immediately replaced with women who soon came to look just like them. It was an awful life for an ignorant woman burdened with far too many children and no dreams left to dream. Writer Hamlin Garland's description of his mother tells the tale:

Her life had been always on the border—she knew nothing of
civilization's splendor of song and story. All her toilsome, monot-
onous days rushed through my mind with a roar, like a file of gray
birds in the night—how little—how tragically small her joys, and
how black her sorrows, her toil, her tedium.

Life on the treeless prairies proved much worse for a woman with a sensitive and emotional nature who couldn't adjust to the frontier way of life. These

Grace and Pete Lemley on their wedding day, March 2, 1898.

types sometimes ended up in insane asylums, or suffered from acute melancholia and were driven to suicide by the emptiness of the land, the winds, and the terrible isolation cut off from their own kind.

But not all pioneer women were wilting Jennies! Far from it. Calamity Jane was a perfect example of another frontier female, the kind of woman no man could tame, full of the devil and part heroine. In Pa's eyes, there were only two types of women, Madonnas and whores and there was nothin' in between. There were wild and dangerous women like Belle Starr, Pearl Hart, and Rose of the Cimarron, but their numbers could be counted on two hands. What happened to all the other millions of red, white, yellow, and black females who inhabited and helped build the American west?

Famed journalist, Nellie Bly, (Elizabeth C. Seaman) went around the world in seventy-two days the year Pa stirred up the Ghost Dancers on the Cheyenne River. Women in more progressive states were becoming doctors and lawyers. They organized suffrage parades and published newspapers but in the new state of South Dakota, whether caught up in their own "Madonna" myths or just too darn busy to care, most western women did what their husbands told them to do and considered they'd made their beds and had to lay in them. Unlike many of her neighbors, Grandma Davis was not an unhappy complainer, nor was she a suffragette leading a parade for equal rights.

Eight years after the Wounded Knee Massacre on a cold March 2, 1898, a little more than a month after the battleship U.S.S. Maine blew up in Havana Harbor, encouraging an outraged American public to demand war with Spain, Lucy and Plummer Davis allowed their lovely daughter Grace, a twenty-one year old with stars in her eyes, to marry Pete Lemley, the Badlands Fox, a man on his way to millions of dollars and many a midnight ride.

The Lemley marriage was a simple ceremony held at high noon in the parlor of Grandpa's Spring Creek ranch, with the Methodist Reverend D. W. Tracy officiating. The bride was radiant, her long hair braided back in a "cadogan" knot with a large white bow of satin ribbon, a regal lavender dress with high-necked white lace bodice scalloped out from shapely shoulders, curving downward to her tiny waist in front. As Mama repeated the wedding vows, her large, adoring eyes following the groom's every gesture, including his sly glance in her direction and a sweep of a knuckle to brush up his mustache. After the ceremony Grandpa Davis hosted a big wedding dinner and Mama found a funny little note from friend Anna Milligen on her plate:

Dear Grace,
Long may you live
And eat good pickles
And marry the man
Who has all the nickles!

In the coming years, despite the enormous amount of nickles Pa earned from the sweat of his brow and the shrewd cunning of his often amoral ways, the permission to marry was a decision Grandma Davis may have lived to regret.

Mama had been teaching school for three years in Black Hawk when it just happened that she received two proposals of marriage on the same day, both in the mail! One letter was from Harry Marshal, a kindly man who would have cherished and protected her for a lifetime. The other was from Pa, no violet bouquets, no champagne or courtship, just a letter that didn't promise lightness and laughter nor elegance and luxury of any kind. He did say, with a mischieviously seductive hint, that he had trained a special pony named "Jolly" to kneel so that a lady of grace could mount side-saddle for romantic evening rides. Grace chose the latter suitor because she was completely enraptured and madly in love with the hero of her girlhood. Among the items in her dowry were twenty-five fat Hereford cows, which grossed Pa $600.00 within three years, a hefty sum at the turn of the century.

Thousands of American women read and re-read a book by woman physician, Dr. P.B. Saur, called *Ideal Womanhood and Motherhood*. The book was highly recommended for all young newly-married women like Mama who believed wholeheartedly in the advice it contained:

> *A wife's life is made up of little pleasures, of little tasks, of little cares, and little duties. . .in sweetening her husband's cup of life. . .The quiet retirement of her home ought to be her greatest pleasure and her most precious privilege.*

It must have been quite a shock from the "little pleasures" when Mama started her married life alone on her honeymoon! Pa wanted to buy horses in the south and afterwards head north to meet Mama at Niagara Falls. During a time when a woman was looked down upon for travelin' across country alone, Mama bravely set out by train for the east, a dangerous adventure for any young girl who had never been out of her own back yard. Pa was off buying horses, enjoying his jaunt across the country, promoting horse buying and puttin' on rodeos, then called "Ropin' and Ridin' Bees". A North Carolina rodeo advertisement featured Pa as the star attraction:

> *LAST CHANCE*
> *A ROPING AND RIDING BEE*
> *Pete Lemley, of Buffalo Bill's Show,*
> *will give a roping and riding Bee at*
> *CATAWBA*
> *He will bring with him a BUCKING BRONCO to show his*
> *riding, he will alone lasso,*
> *THROW and TIE a HORSE*

in less time than one minute. He is certainly as good a roper as is
on earth to-day and the most fearless rider known in the West.
COME AND SEE HIM.
Very truly, J. W. Blackwelder

Meanwhile, Mama set off alone on her honeymoon trip with the cheapest train ticket, sleepin' in her seat next to greasy traveling salesmen and large families with tired cranky babies, bundles, and boxes. She couldn't afford the dining car, instead she bought fruit, jam, and bread from vendors at railroad depots along the way. She didn't eat much anyway, and her tiny five foot frame could get by with one meal a day if need be. The route from Rapid City took her to Chicago, Illinois, and through Cleveland, Ohio, huge cities with more people than she'd ever seen in one place at a time. With little space for luggage, she was forced to sit on top of her belongings, hopelessly wrinkling her special outfit, the dress she wanted to wear when she stepped off the train in Buffalo, New York, into the arms of her anxiously awaitin' bridegroom.

Mama could hardly wait. From the train window she watched the prairies flyin' by, then more trees and family farms nestled in hills, to dark forests, more beautiful than she had ever imagined. The long days and longer nights passed by slowly, then monotonously, until one early morning the train lurched and clanged into Buffalo, New York, its final destination, just twenty-two miles from the powerful Niagara. Mother stood by the door with her suitcase in hand, pushed and shoved along as she tried to recognize her husband among the waiting crowd.

The straw hat, straight blue skirt and gingham blouse with bouncy leg-of-mutton sleeves turned out to be her honeymoon suit. The fancy dress in the flattened suitcase wasn't fit to wear. She had spent her last cent on food the evening before and it was reassurin' to know Pa would be there to take care of her at the train station. Mama finally emerged from the train and walked out into the sunlight on the long green platform. She looked up and down; he must be trying to fool her. She slowly walked to the depot, children running past, dogs barking and porters scrambling by with heavy luggage piled on moving carts. There were so many people, carriages, horses; perhaps she had missed him back at the train. She retraced her steps only to find the train pullin' away with great gushes of noisy steam.

The lonely realization that Pa wasn't there to meet her took a few minutes to sink in. When it did, Mother drifted into a momentary sadness but came out of it quickly enough when she felt her stomach growling. There was only one thing to do. She took up her suitcase, straightened her coat and hat, and walked downtown, head held high as if she knew exactly what she was doing. Mama saw the huge white bank building from two blocks away. She walked very purposely right into the bank and asked to speak to the bank president! Before she knew it, she was ushered into his impressive office, a large open room with a

The 1890s.

great marble fireplace, Greek statuary, and heavy dark curtains on windows from ceiling to floor. The president came in and properly introduced himself to the pretty young stranger.

There were no bewildered looks, no pitiful tears, no scene of any kind. Mama matter-of-factly told the banker that her husband was late picking her up from a horse-buying trip in the south and she needed a loan until he got there. Perhaps her beauty helped some, the banker was only too happy to be of service, in fact, had she had breakfast yet? He was just on his way to have a bite and he would enjoy "an honest face" at breakfast.

Pa finally got to Buffalo a week later. Mother had spent many hours in the Public Library, pouring over much beloved books, waitin' for her husband to show up. She walked around Buffalo, saw the magnificent buildings, the cozy homes in the evenings, dim lights blinking behind window curtains, the homes she was sure, of happily married couples raising sweet children. For many years afterward, she wrote little appreciative notes to a certain banker in Buffalo at Christmas. By the time Mama got to see Niagara Falls, it wasn't quite as romantic as she thought it would be.

Shortly after they returned from the honeymoon trip, Pa up and left again on another horse-buyin' trip, leaving mother stuck in a log cabin on the Cheyenne River, the only real ground that he owned at the time. A few days later, with no warning, the Cheyenne flooded its banks a half-mile wide. Before Mama could leave the cabin for higher ground, water ran in and around the few pieces of oak furniture in the one-room cabin. With quiet calm, she opened the door and the one small window, climbed up on the kitchen table with a pile of fancywork and waited it out. The water rose higher and higher until it was just nearly level with the table top. Her belongings began floating around her, pots, pans, and now and again one of her favorite books! But Mama could only embroider, unable to move for fear the soggy table legs would give way. Water lapped over the table top and soaked her skirt and she held her embroidery up a little higher. She said a few prayers and sang a loud hymn hoping someone might hear, but Mama saw humor in her predicament instead of total despair. "Every once in awhile a little muscrat swam through to keep me company," she later recalled, and the sweet, funny bewhiskered faces greeting her as they paddled past, gave her courage. The sun went down and she waited in the darkness, a tiny cold figure huddled and shivering. The moon was completely hidden by clouds, occasionally something living splashed by and Mother was thankful that if it were a rat, at least she could not see it. Her thoughts drifted to her mother and father, and her husband, the man she depended upon to feed, clothe and protect her. Oh, how much better a wife she would try to be if only she could stay awake and live through this, for sleep might surely mean a watery grave. As the first rays of sunlight appeared, Mama saw that although her clothing was soaked, and her shoes had floated away, the waters had finally started to recede. By noon, she was able to climb up to the roof to watch the river back away, taking with it almost everything of value, includin' Pa's woodpile.

With no telephone, radio, electricity or neighbors Mama spent endless days and nights alone. It was especially frightening at night when the snow drifted up past the doorlatch and the wind howled through cracks leaving little piles of snow on the bed quilts in the morning. Mama was the eternal optimist, always seein' the best of everyone and never despairing of someday, in some significant way, changing the tiger's stripes. After all, didn't her book say, "A cheerful, happy temper. . .often converts an indifferent or absent husband into a good one." Grandma Davis had been willing to let her daughter marry because Pa "kept a good woodpile," and as it turned out, a very big pile of wood was just about the only thing that kept Mama warm on many a night.

Salaries for hired men were very low, often just room and board for a drifter passing through. Pa finally had to break down and hire several of them to build and repair fences, buildings, and ride for strays, which was the main consideration in addition to breaking saddle horses and working teams. Mother got along by herself in the dark log cabin, washing and cooking for squads of men on an old wood cook stove, to say nothing of caring for thirteen hunting dogs that required washtubs full of cornmeal mush. Her days were filled with the dreaded, back-breaking wash, chinking, daubing, and stripping off the bark from the inside cabin walls, making butter and cheese, tending chickens, putting up jellies and vegetables, making candle molds and soap, and many other chores. Sandra L. Myers in *Westering Women* describes the labor involved in washing clothes for twenty men:

1. *Build fire in back yard to heat kettles of rain water.*
2. *Set tubs so smoke won't blow in eyes.*
3. *Shave whole cakes of lye soap in boiling water.*
4. *Sort things. make three large piles. 1 pile white, 1 pile colored, 1 pile work britches and rags.*
5. *Stir flour in cold water to smooth, then thin down with boilin' water for starch.*
6. *Rub dirty spots on board, scrub hard. Then boil. Rub colored but don't boil, just rinse, wring, and starch.*
7. *Take white things out of kettle with broom stick handle, then rinse, wring, . . .and starch.*
8. *Pour rinse water out.*
9. *Scrub porch with left over soupy water.*
10. *Turn tubs upside down.*
11. *Go put on a clean dress, smooth hair with side combs, brew cup of tea, rest and rock a spell and count blessings.*

Mama counted herself fortunate to have more than one tub, and a scrub board. Before washing, she had to make soap. Some women bought their lye, but more often they made their own by pouring water and lime through fireplace ashes carefully kept for this purpose. The lye was then mixed with the leftover household grease, which was also kept in a barrel or can. The lye and the grease were boiled together and constantly stirred until the soap "came" and was then dipped into the soap barrel. This smelly chore was usually done outdoors in the blowing wind, ashes sticking like glue to arms and clothing, and sparks covering skirts and exposed skin. With the soap made, water had to be hauled and the real work began. Some women remarked that wash day was "the day I detest above all others," and another said she was so tired of washing she felt "worse than a stewed witch."

Mother often felt tired and sad but she remembered the advice given to young women:

> *The first maxim which you should impress deeply upon your mind is never to attempt to control your husband by opposition, by displeasure, or any mark of anger. . .If he be a good man, he expects from you smiles, not frowns. Besides, what can a woman gain by opposition or indifference? Nothing; but she loses everything. She loses her husband's respect for her. She loses his love, and with that all prospect of future happiness.*

Therefore, it was always a cheerful, glowing face and a pretty smile that met Pa every time he returned home from the range. She often had Pa's favorite donuts and fresh apple pies, boiled chicken and dumplings, gravy and biscuits. Although Mama always called her husband "Pete" or sometimes "Mr.," he never called her by her given name, but referred to his wife throughout their married lives as "the Missus," partially no doubt to keep the hired men from ever calling her anything but "Missus Lemley."

Pa worked hard at the Circle Bar ranch, adding horses (one way or the other.) He was always downright stingy with his money, saved every cent of his salary, and hardly ever went to town with the boys to spend his hard-earned cash. Of course, he rarely allowed Mama to go to town either, and she was never given spending money. He continued buying stock in the Circle Bar, owned by directors, J.R. McGrew and Mr. Rhodes. McGrew owned half-interest in the Baltimore and Ohio Railroad and several other businesses. Pa said, "There were a a lot of people from the east had horse ranches out on the Cheyenne. There were horse ranches every ten to fifteen miles, Englishmen, Italians, all kinds of foreign fellas in there. I was handlin' pureblooded horses and a trackin' 'em; mares, keepin' dates an' things so I could register them. Had a lot of stallions; twenty-one with Ben Hur the trottin' horse. He was a Hamiltonian, a fast horse. They paid six thousand dollars for him, a lot of money in them days out in Lexington, Kentucky. They ended up with 900 head." He did not mention how many he ended up with, but he always knuckled his mustache when he talked of it.

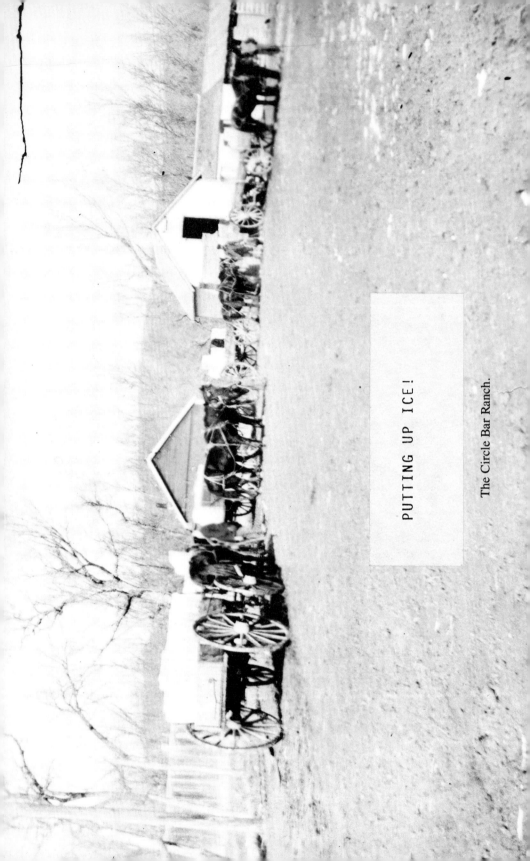

PUTTING UP ICE!

The Circle Bar Ranch.

There came a time in 1897, when the owners woke up to find that Pa owned more stock in their company than they did! They sold out to him and with part of their money bought themselves a nice new automobile, which they had to leave on the creek bank because there wasn't a bridge for it. A flash flood came along and whoosh! It floated down the creek, much to Pa's everlasting amusement.

He was now the proud owner of the Circle Bar. Unhindered by barbed wire, or settler's threats, he ran as many as 1,500 horses at a time from the Belle Fourche River to the Little Missouri. Once he saddled up a big old bronc, left Ft. Pierre at 3 a.m. and pulled into his ranch on the Cheyenne the next morning. To add insult to injury, he had to swim the river as it had flooded while he was gone. Pa was never troubled by boredom, his workaholic nature was dedicated to just one thing, the advancement of Pete Lemley's worldly goods, and with this attitude, he was perfectly happy to take a few days off here and there as long as he could do it on his horse.

Grace welcomed visitors while Pa was gone, some of which he would not have approved. Ma's door was always open when Indians came from the reservation to the annual 4th of July Round-up at Belle Fourche, bringing with them all their wagons, teams, and families, Mama baked many loaves of delicious bread for them. When the caravans got to the ranch, they usually went up into the pastures to dig for wild turnips and Mama often invited the ladies for dinner. The Lakota women wore big brightly colored shawls, and after they had eaten, they spread out the shawls, gathered up leftovers for their children and Mama added all the beautiful loaves of homemade bread and pails of milk. After the round-up, on the return trip, they stopped again and Mother would repeat her generous hospitality. Every so often she found a little beaded present on the doorstep. They had not forgotten her.

Early ranchers, settlers, and cowboys didn't quite look on Indians as human beings, more like something to destroy if the occasion presented itself, which it often did. The sport of huntin' Indians was much like huntin' elk. There were some whitemen who didn't count themselves men unless they'd killed an Indian. For years after the real fightin' was over, the old-timers pulled out their Indian scalps to tell their tales and show off, much like the Indians did with white scalps. A treaty didn't mean a damn thing to a rancher, miner, or homesteader looking for gold or land for his family, just as it meant nothing to George Armstrong Custer when he came to the Black Hills in "74".

After the Ghost Dance excitement, Pa never went in for killing any more Indians. He didn't understand people of other races and was confounded by them. He used to tell a joke on himself (one of the few). He was in North Carolina buyin' horses and he needed a crew to build a corral and chutes so he and another fella could put on one of their ridin' and ropin' rodeos. The Southerners were real hospitable people and fixed him up with what they called a "nigger crew." He got them all together and went to showin' them how he wanted the corral. The logs were to be placed just so. . .the notching like this. . .pretty soon he'd done a couple of them and he looked around and the crew had all run off! Seems they'd work FOR a whiteman but not WITH a whiteman! He thought that was a strange kind of snobbery. He did admit that the best horse wrangler he ever hired was an enormous black man who almost equalled the horses in sheer strength.

As the years went by, Mama realized that if she were ever to have anything of her own, she'd have to find a way to earn it without leavin' the ranch. Everyone commented on her beautiful fancywork and it was the fancywork money that bought her first sewing machine. Now, at least, she could make herself a dress or two as soon as she earned enough for material. She was always afraid to ask Pa for anything because he didn't like to spend a penny! She gathered up all her courage one day and told him that she was savin' her fancywork money and had worked her fingers raw making hand muffs from muscrat skins. She explained that she wanted to open a little savings account at the bank for household expenses and for a future trip to see his sister Libby Morgan in Oregon. "What?" he growled, "The hell you are! No woman in my house is ever goin' to open up no God damn such thing! All the money goes to my bank account, every damn last penny as long as you live!" And that was the end of it. Mama felt so ashamed to have asked him, she later wrote to Libby:

> *Pete doesn't like me to have a separate account so will turn the $100 in to pay for my trip out west and buy a rocking chair with the $15.00 and sit and rock the rest of the year. I am wild to go to the coast, but expect to get tame again before the chance comes to go.*

THE 20TH CENTURY ON THE CHEYENNE

istory and time passed in America to the year 1898, when President William McKinley asked Congress to declare war against Spain, after the American battleship Maine was blown up in Havana harbor, killing two hundred and sixty American seamen. Most Americans were riled up over the loss of the Maine but Pa saw only dollar signs when war threatened. The year before he sold six hundred horses to the British during the Boer War and now was buyin' up all the horses he could find for the Spanish American War. Teddy Roosevelt made the "Rough Riders" famous and good mounts were hard to come by.

Mother wrote to Libby that Pa "sprained his ankle going over a fence and he can't bear to be disabled. The wolves have gotten to his colts, killing many of them—so he went out with a pack of hounds and shot seven wolves in one day." He sprained his ankle on a barbed wire fence, one of many that were startin' to go up all over the place. Pa hated the barbed wire and the men who broke up his miles and miles of open range. Nothing was more exasperating than to have six hundred horses out in front and suddenly have the lead horse caught in barbed wire, legs flailing, screamin' in pain, the rest stampedin' in all directions—all hell breaking loose!

The Spanish American War was soon over but Pa didn't care—he'd made a wagon-load of money. Not many people saw the handwriting on the wall in 1899 when President McKinley became the first president to ride in a noisy new fangled contraption called an automobile, a Stanley Steamer, scarin' women and children, spooking horses and generally causing a lot of unfavorable discussion about the foolish invention most said would never last. Nothing important ever happened anywhere else than on Pa's ranch and he could have cared less about any new noisy machines. Horses were all he cared about. Pa always liked to tell the story of a cowboy named Joe who'd been out on the range when along came another cowboy ridin' hard. He reined up and shouted, "Joe, McKinley's been shot!" Joe looked puzzled, scratched his head, and asked, "McKinley. . . McKinley? What outfit is he with?" Pa hadn't been at the Rapid City Grand Ballroom of the Harney Hotel the night the town went wild when McKinley was elected. When McKinley was shot, Pa and Joe kept on ridin'. It was just another day on the range.

A new century dawned in America, one that would bring greater changes in a shorter period of time than Pa ever imagined. By 1900, Americans talked to each other over one million telephones. Within fifteen years, they rode in automobiles and airplanes, purchased electric vacuum cleaners, stoves, fans, irons, refrigerators and washing machines, radios, and phonographs; wonderful machines for use in the home and in the workplace. But not in Pete Lemley's home or workplace. Not on your life! Just a waste of good money on all this new, expensive foolishness.

Mama's tiny hands and feet were never idle. She cooked and baked for as many as twenty ranch hands, three meals a day, did their washing by hand, sewed and mended all the clothes and only found a moment to herself when she read a few words from her books by lamplight. In 1900, she gave birth to a sweet little red-haired girl, Mable, but her own body was so worn out that the baby was weakened and died in her mother's arms when just a few weeks old. Mother mourned the death of her first child quietly, confiding to her sister in law, "So do we all get old all at once." She had been alone most of the time of her pregnancy and confinement and during the birth. On her birthday, while Pa was in Ohio, her mother came unexpectedly to see her, "I never was so glad to see anybody as I was then," she wrote.

One of Pa's favorite ways to make quick money was bettin' on the horse races at the county fair. Young fellas followed Pa around knowing that whichever horse he bet on was a sure thing. One day in Rapid City he and a friend went to see how much they could win. In those days, the winnings were paid in silver dollars so Pa took along a couple of empty bags, slung them over his shoulder and went to the races. By the end of the day, he had so much silver he could hardly lift the bags. He tied one bag to a friend's saddle and one to his own and off they went for home. They'd only gone a little ways when Pa suddenly reined up and listened. He was always aware of sounds, almost like a sixth sense. He got off his horse and put his ear to the ground. They'd been goin' east down the valley, the usual way home, but now he motioned his friend to follow and he turned off to the breaks south of Rapid Creek. Sure enough, it wasn't long before two strange riders come sneakin' by following their trail. When they were out of danger, Pa got off his horse, took the bags and opened them up on the ground. He counted $800 in silver coin, enough to make any greasy highway robber a happy man. Pa's ability to sense danger paid off many times in his life and he never trusted anyone, ever. He had an uncanny way of reading the character of a man after just a few minutes; he knew men almost as well as he knew horses.

In 1902, Mother delivered a healthy baby boy she named Ray and now, besides the multitude of chores was the added responsibility of the child. A slight change came over Mama, the old enthusiasm for life began to fade and her letters to Aunt Libby took on a new tone:

I chase after the baby, scrub and wash, and cook for men until my wits are one continuous jumble, no chance to go "wool-gathering" as wits are said to do. I am 26 years old today. . .some days I feel like it was a hundred. . .Hope we won't always live here, though I take pride in knowing I have never complained. . .No use to nag a man to change and then get the credit of making him 'go broke.

Pa was considered one of the wealthiest men in the region but he absolutely refused to fix anything at the cabin. Since women and their concerns took second place to practically everything, a nice house was not part of Pa's plan. Mother finally got fed up with cooking for hordes of men and as many hounds in a one-room log cabin with one window and only one door—cross ventilation was impossible. She was supposed to have dinner served piping hot whenever the men got back from the range and that could mean anywhere from noon to three o'clock, She had to be vigilant listening for the jingle of harness and the creak of wagon wheels in order to whisk food on the table before it dried up or got cold. On one typically masculine occasion, a big crew came to dinner, piling into the small log cabin lickin' their chops. Mother was rocking placidly (quaking inwardly) and she just kept on rockin' back and forth, back and forth. The men were fallin' all over each other looking for the usual spread of meat and potatoes, pies, fresh biscuits, and gravy. Mother just kept on rockin'. No sir, if someone didn't get busy and produce two windows and another door, there wasn't goin' to be any dinner! It didn't take very long with a bunch of hungry men on the business ends of a saw and axe until there was cross ventilation in the stifling heat. The dinner was whisked out of various hiding places, and everybody was happy. It was forty miles by team and buggy to a piece of glass, but it was all in place by the time the snow started to fly. "You would be shocked to see our manner of living," Mama confided to Libby:

Now after people have hoarded up that much besides a wad in the bank, don't you think they ought to have a spree, once in awhile? I would dislike worse than being poor, to be miserly & not enjoy spending something. Between you and me, he has this malady bad.

Mother always made such delicious food. Beef was the staple meat and Pa raised a few pigs which supplied all the lard ever used, the sausages were cooked and stored in stone crocks. Pa cured the hams himself, soaking them in his own brine recipe and then smoking them over a slow ash fire for days. The summer hay crews of nineteen or twenty men had reason to be thankful for Pa's smoked hams and Mother's old wood stove. Pa was even happier when fish was the main menu. He completely disdained sitting on a bank with a fishing pole. His idea of fishin' was to get a bunch of neighbors and all their kids, and have a fun-filled day seining deep holes in the creek. For the daily amount of fish needed to pro-

Members of the Fancyworks Club.

vide meals for the hay crew, Pa relied on a fish trap set in the old swimmin' hole every night after the hay crew had exhausted themselves with a much needed bath. The huge catfish, eight and nine pound giants, were a regular feast when skinned and cut sideways like pork chops. Nothing pleased Pa more than this delicious fare, and besides, it was cheaper! After a few years it became illegal to set a fish trap, but this silly law didn't stop Pa for a minute. The creek ran through his land, and he had always eaten the fish in it. Later on, someone reported Pa to the game warden and at this treacherous point in time, the fish trap happened to be resting on the creek bank. The game warden brought the unmistakable evidence up to the ranch. Pa was carrying his trusty old rifle, and he forcibly set the butt on the ground and with great indignation roared, "Son, that's my turkey crate, and you're on my land! I'll give you just thirty seconds to get the Hell off!" When the dust cleared, the game warden was gone, and the turkey crate went back to the creek bank. Try as he might, Pa never did catch a turkey in that creek.

While Pa was havin' his fun, Mama nearly forgot how to laugh. After years of marriage bottled up with sand burrs, primitive living conditions and hard work, lifting heavy buckets of water, scrubbing rough wood floors, cleaning smoked glass chimneys for kerosene lamps, carryin' in dirty armfuls of wood, the many chores of life on the Cheyenne took their toll:

> *The world wags on whether we mix in the throng and accomplish some good to others or become absorbed in thoughts of what we eat and wear, and our own selfishness. The world is not concerned over what we make of ourselves, is it? But I tell you the right kind of people are those who see the pleasures and don't care much whether the floor is swept or not before they can laugh at a joke or tell a funny story. They are thought of most highly, while the scrub-adub-dubs are sadly out of it. I am mentally kicking myself for being of this second class and a victim of surroundings. No church, society, or anything to break the monotony. . .Well I must mix my staff of life and go to bed. I can't run down to the bake shop and get two loaves for a nickel. I weigh 103 pounds.*

Mama was a social creature and she decided the only way to cure loneliness was to start a fancywork club. She called the first meeting and was surprised when forty wretched creatures drove God knows how many miles to get there! They pulled their wagons up to the ranch, reined in with dust flyin' and climbed down. All walked quietly up to the door, their skin parched and dry, wispy hair falling from rows of coil-braided heads, half pinned; faded calico and linsey woolsey dresses and babies clutched to their breasts. They stood there tired and silent, looking dumbstruck at each other, having utterly forgotten the socialization and fun of their youth. Mama scurried around introducin' people and

The Log Cabin on the Cheyenne River. Pa, Mama, and Ray with their dog — 1901.

merrily produced quilts to spread on the ground in front of the cabin. She wasn't prepared for so many. Several of the women helped and before long tea and cookies were served to the ladies of the fancywork club, the first time in years that some had been served by others, had allowed themselves the time to sit down and talk about themselves, had relaxed from the ruthless tasks of their lives to reach out for the comfort only another woman friend could provide.

Mama couldn't help comparing herself to these women, the telltale bruises on their arms and faces, some heavy with child holding another not yet a year old. It took awhile before there was so much as a shy half-smile, but Mama would have none of that! She stood up in front of them all and gave a little speech about why she thought the fancywork club was a good idea. There was no use doing fancywork alone when they could all meet once a month and have a few hours of lively conversation was there? And one or another of the ladies might want to share recipes or health care remedies, or maybe give a report on something interesting? Why yes, they could all bring their catalogues, a rare newspaper or magazine, and share a topic with the group? Suddenly, there was a smile, a peel of laughter in the grim, calicoed group, and the ice was broken at last. What followed was the most awfully noisy three hours Mama had ever heard! The women talked incessantly, as if they had never talked before, sippin' tea with cracked, dried hands more used to washing clothes in icy cold or steamin' hot water than liftin' china teacups. When the meeting was over, friendships were made and it was a smiling, happier group of ladies who took the reins and headed for home over miles and miles of winding dirt paths that led back to their monotonous, hard lives. And Mama went back to hers as well. In 1904 she wrote Libby:

I have thought of you a great deal lately, but only when the baby is asleep for that is the only opportunity I have for thought. He is two years old now, and so full of mischief. He killed all my little chickens until we made a tight wire fence to put all the coops in and now he skins through that, which is rather hard on his clothes. He is always into something!. . .O we never any of us repaid our mothers for the care and trouble we caused did we?. . .Aren't you ashamed to live on the fat of the land, while your sister is lodged along the sandy Cheyenne River without a fruit or vegetable to lay her jaws to?. . .I would like to live where things grow.

Every time Mother mentioned taking a little trip, even to town, Pa would decide to buy more land. This was his best evasion technique:

Pete. . .went a little in to buy four more ranches this Spring. But he will never get where he couldn't see out by standing on his toes, and will be all right as soon as he makes a sale. We have branded about

a hundred and thirty colts and have a good many more to brand yet.
Must be over 400 and we have one hundred thirty cattle.

Mother had been reading the newspapers lent by the fancywork club and she spent some of her own money on a subscription to the new magazine "Good Housekeeping." From studying, she learned that the economy of the west was changing and Pa wasn't. She summoned all her courage again and had a little talk with Pa after he had eaten a good dinner one evening. Men are always in better spirits after a meal, as every smart woman in the world knows. She told him that people were supplementing their horse herds with cattle because the day was coming when the horseless automobiles would be more useful than horses in towns and maybe even in the country. Banks Stewart, a candy salesman from Deadwood, made a sensation when he drove a locomobile down main street in Rapid City. Howell Clenger bought a single cylinder Oldsmobile and someone had even seen a Winton that carried five passengers. A Mr. Leedy had a vehicle called a Yale with a finished wood body like a piano, kerosene headlights made of brass and tubeless tires. It went twenty miles per hour! But the best was an elongated bed on an automobile that could be used to haul wood and furniture at a much faster rate than a team.

Pa puffed on his pipe—pretended he wasn't listening. Of course, it was months before Mama found out he had taken her advice and bought over a hundred cattle. It must have given her a secret feeling of accomplishment, especially when the day came when cars and high priced pasture made it impossible to continue raising huge horse herds.

In *Good Housekeeping* Mama read that "Sensible and responsible women do not want to vote." This was Grover Cleveland writing, "The relative positions to be assumed by men and women in the working out of our civilization were assigned long ago by a higher intelligence than ours." So it must have been God Himself who decided women weren't as intelligent as men? She also read about an English suffragist, Emmeline Pankhurst who was willing to use arson, bombing, and hunger strikes to gain the vote for women. Suffrage and the vote meant next to nothing to a ranch woman on the Cheyenne. Still, when the chores and cooking were done and mother fell exhausted into bed, she began to think about it.

THE NIGHTRIDER

In many areas of the west vigilante groups often crossed the line that separated lawful from lawless, a common but unpublicized practice in the smaller South Dakota towns and settlements. Some settlers, and Indian agents, carried titles such as "Major" or "Captain," many of them men who never actually served in uniform but covered their checkered past lives with false Civil War exploits. Cavalry deserters, robbers, killers or irresponsible men runnin' away from unwanted wives and children back east became instant "Colonels." These men never talked much about their past even to their western friends and families. It was easy for a man wanted for murder in Pennsylvania to drop out of existence only to surface wearing a beard or mustache in South Dakota with a new last like Allen, Miller, Ford, Powers, Clark, West, Smith, or Jones; something easy to spell. If they were quiet and tried to fit in, they could be founding fathers of new towns in the west, become pillars of the community, hold positions of respect in churches, school boards, banks, and once in awhile they might even make Sheriff or Marshal. Pa grew up consorting with the likes of Jesse James and he didn't have much use for counterfeit colonels or men who pretended to be what they were not.

As a large landowner, Pa held an enviable position along the Cheyenne. People didn't know whether to hate or love him, but they respected Pa enough to stay clear of him unless there was a crisis. When a man needed advice in a dangerous situation Pa made himself available. The Federal Marshals and Sheriffs were usually too weak-livered to do much good during the many feuds that developed over land claims, and fights between sheep herders and cattlemen.

The Folsom Feud, a famous quarrel around the area, started when the Stucker family came swaggering into Folsom with new tractors and took over the J-D place at Cheyenne Flat, on land that was owned by Charles Seaman of Hermosa and W.C. Nisson of Aberdeen. The Stuckers were troublemakers from the beginning, dividing the ranchers into sympathizers and enemies when once they had all been neighbors. Stucker planted flax right on the Cheyenne Flats in the middle of cow country. Now there were herd laws and fence laws but most folks just helped each other out when a cow wandered into somebody's field. Stucker, however, made the fatal mistake of rounding up all the cows that wandered into his unfenced flax and he held them for damages. He drove them up to a ranch on Spring Creek, about ten miles west of the J-D place. Meanwhile, Eugene Milton, a Stucker sympathizer, shut up a bunch of horses belonging to the Bradfords. In the dead of night, a mysterious rider from the Cheyenne River rode up and let the cattle out of the corral and then the Bradford boys later crawled into the corral and let their horses out. That should have ended it, but Stucker called the Custer County Sheriff, Tom Fenwick. Cattle got mixed up in several different herds, hot arguments ensued, and shots rang out. This went on for years, back and forth, with the mysterious Nightrider making his appearance whenever Stucker rounded up horses or cattle for damages. The Custer County Sheriff came down numerous times but the Nightrider always outrode whomever was on his trail, and it was rumored that the mysterious man was a resident of Pennington County so the Custer County Sheriff couldn't do a thing, or was too afraid to cross the line.

Finally, one night Reed Stucker heard a noise outside and went out with his gun to see what it was. He found two men on horseback. One man fired a single shot, hitting him in the arm. While Reed was recovering from his wound, another shooting occurred at the Ed Peterson place. Clarence Stucker was chased to the house by two masked men who then rode around blasting out the windows. The terrified kid hit the floor and crawled across the kitchen to the telephone. He telephoned the operator and she found his dad who was about twelve miles away. Stucker told his son to clear out and come home at once. Nearly everyone on the party line heard the frightened conversation. The boy dropped the phone clanging against the wall and ran out to the barn leaving the telephone operator yelling into the phone, "Clarence are you there? Please answer me!" The only thing she could hear was the terrible sound of twenty-five people breathin' heavily.

When the boy got to the barn he found the animals kicking wildly in their stalls, frightened at the crashing gunfire. He jumped on his horse and took off. No sooner had he left, when he turned to see two riders gainin' on him. The first shots whizzed over his head and he kicked his horse on. Pchew! Faster, faster. He ducked. Pchew! Another shot rang out. It was a wild race for miles over gullies and creeks. Although at least one rider was an expert marksman and could have killed the kid with one shot, the men decided it was a lot more fun to scare him to death instead. The Sheriff was again called in but he couldn't find a clue.

The outraged cattlemen met again with the Nightrider for advice on what they should do to get rid of the Stuckers once and for all! The sly fox reportedly knuckled his mustache. "Well, God Almighty," he said, "Hit them in their wallet pocket where it hurts." Several nights later, just as the flax was ready to be harvested, a lone fox, very rare in those parts, watched from a nearby hill as Stucker's entire flax harvest went up in flames. The mysterious fire started about midnight and the glow could be seen ten miles away. The damage was reported at about $7,500 and folks said that since it was such a clear night without a bolt of lightning in the sky, then it must have been Stucker who burned his own flax!

Stucker sued a couple of men for slander asking $10,000 damages and for a time seemed to have all the newspapers on his side. News stories reported there certainly were a bunch of hard-ridin' outlaws around. Stucker's lawsuit fell apart when folks found out that he had written a book entitled *The Silent Riders Of The Night* and the last chapter was unfinished except the outcome of the trial. The jury returned a verdict against Stucker and he high-tailed it out of the country and hasn't been back since. Small crime, big results were more Pa's cup of tea.

Another time an old Swede named Ole Johnson ran five miles barefoot through cactus that would have stopped a horse to get to Pa's ranch for help. He was reputed to have hidden a big sack of money somewhere on his homestead and one day a group of men who were not at all particular how they acquired money, horses, guns or anything of value, rode in and tried to persuade Ole to tell them where he had hidden his money. He refused and they left him tied to a wagon wheel. They figured a day or two in the broiling sun without water would change his mind. Somehow, the slippery Swede got loose and since they had taken his shoes, he ran barefoot to Pete Lemley for help. Pa saddled up a horse for Ole and rode back with him to the old man's cabin, his Colt .45 fairly tingling in its holster. If the men came back, nobody ever heard what became of them.

There were some, though, who didn't think Pa was too neighborly. A man about the same age as Pa, an early settler who shared thousands of acres of free government pasture for a decade or more right alongside Pa, ended up tellin' folks he was going to, "dance on Pete Lemley's grave." When the rights of way were being purchased for railroad tracks Pa had his ear to the ground enough to hear the singing of the rails (or the singing of the cash register). He bought up a big tract of land from the neighbor on the south side of the Lemley ranch and he paid what the neighbor considered a "helluva good price." Well, he should have known better because Pa never paid anybody a good price. Before the neighbor quit congratulating himself on gettin' rid of those worthless gumbo acres, which weren't much good for anything anyway, here come the railroad officials of the Chicago, Milwaukee and St. Paul Railroad! They were willing to pay a small fortune for the land he had just sold to Pa. The neighbor never got over it. When Pa told the story he was always a little puzzled, "I can't understand why he got so mad, and why in Hell he couldn't hear that train chuggin' over the prairie just as loud as I could!" Years later, the neighbor died and Pa bought the whole ranch from his widow. First thing Pa did after the sale was dance a little jig on his friend's grave.

Pa was trailing horses with another fellow, accumulating their herd to sell to the armies, and they camped for the night and picketed the horses. During the night something happened to the picket security, and the horses wandered off.

Just cracking dawn revealed to the searching eyes the horses grazing contently in what appeared to be a field of very tall grass which turned out to be a wheat field almost ready to harvest. While Pa and partner were hurrying the horses away, a buggy appeared in the distance.

The partner told Pa to go calm the man down and pay him for damages to his wheat field. It was not the dreaded owner of the field, but a man wanting to buy a team of horses. Pa sold him the team for a fair price, put the money in his pocket and reported to his partner that he "had a terrible time with that irate wheat farmer, and had to give him the horses to calm him down!" Everybody was happy. . .the horse partner that the damages weren't more costly, Pa snug with the money in his pocket, and the man who bought the horses getting a pretty good deal. The wheat farmer was probably the only one who felt abused.

After another little boy, Chauncey, joined the Lemley household in 1910, Pa found yet another way to make money. Homesteaders, many of them from Iowa, came to South Dakota where they envisioned the vast, rolling prairies as future fields of waving grain. Pa might have helped those visions out a bit when he met homesteaders as they arrived by train. Brimming with enthusiasm, they stayed at our house until Pa could put one of his old shacks on skids and pull it off to a tract of land he sold to the homesteaders. Sometimes he'd even outfit them with wagons, teams, harness, and equipment depending on how much money he found out they had. The homesteaders planted wheat and their crops were nearly ripe when nature or other mysterious nocturnal happenings began to occur. If it wasn't grasshoppers, it was cut fences, if it wasn't blizzards or drought, it was phantom cows trampling crops. One way or another they were ready to throw in the sponge after one season. Since Pa was just about the only affluent man nearby, he'd go over and offer, out of the pure goodness of his heart, to buy back everything he'd sold them in the first place. Of course, used equipment and harder times meant he couldn't pay them too much, but at that point they'd take anything just to get the hell out of the country. For years, the Lemley family used articles which retained the owner's names, and the fields were always referred to as the "Nolin Field," the "Keliher Place," or the "Ellison Draw." It got so that Pa went to the train depot quite a bit and just left the old shack on the skids. After sellin' out to Pa, one farmer went back to the shack and fell asleep. He must have been drunk because Pa started pulling the shack back late the next day, got about ten feet and the farmer poked his head out of the door: "Can't you waittt till I gettt out?" he stammered. The wonderful custom of designating areas by some original owner's name still persists. After all, it gives a delightful sense of immortality; the only one those courageous and ill-fated people ever had. Added to this, the nice bonus Pa got by acquiring 30,000 acres of pasture land.

It was along about this time that Mr. Bergman, a German with an accent so thick one could mimic him with great results, went in with Pa to lease a huge area in the Badlands for summer pasture. For years they pastured together, made the drives down and back (25 miles) with seasonal regularity, and became good friends in spite of the usual devastating practical jokes that lightened the tedium. Sometimes the jokes got so out of hand that hard feelings resulted. Mr. Bergman was a wealthy gentleman who had divorced his first wife, homely as a hedge fence, but solid gold, in order to marry a stylish young widow with a beautiful daughter. The ex-Mrs. Bergman was forced to take a job as governess in Sioux Falls. Mama felt so sorry for her that she visited the poor woman for many years afterward.

The first Mrs. Bergman had given the best years of her life to a man who threw her off like an old blanket. She hadn't a penny after the divorce so she went to work as governess for a widower with two motherless children. She ended up marrying him, but she remembered her first husband all the rest of her life and often asked Mother about him. Mr. Bergman had inherited a fortune from his uncle according to Pa, but he lost the fortune largely due to the fact that his second wife wanted a huge new house with the unheard-of extravagance of $800 worth of curtains! On top of that the second Mrs. Bergman thought cowhands on roundups should be fed well so she sent along cans of vegetables and peaches! This horrified my father, who saw the caverns of insolvency yawning right inside the empty peach cans! Mr. Bergman built a magnificent house for his new bride, six bedrooms, formal butler's pantry, a separate dining room just for the hired men! Pa thought this wildly extravagant and began predicting Mr. Bergman's financial ruin. Sure enough, someone offered to buy the house for a big chunk of money and the Bergmans moved out. The man reneged on the deal right during a hard drought and Mr. Bergman lost everything! Through poor management, slow markets, drought and Mrs. Bergman's curtains and peaches, they were left destitute. Mother never stopped hearing about the $800 curtains to the end of her days! Every time Mama wanted a little something to brighten up the cabin, Pa brought up those curtains.

While the bank was foreclosing on Mr. Bergman, Pa convinced the banker to hold off the proceedings until Fall. The cattle would be fatter, the calves bigger, and the market couldn't do anything but go up. The verbal agreement with the banker was that the bank would pay half the cost of the rental on the summer pasture, which amounted to about $300 apiece. Pa paid his half of the rental payment and the summer wore on. With Fall coming on Pa went to visit the banker and to collect Mr. Bergman's share of the rent. The banker refused to pay up, mumbling there had been no written agreement. Pa threatened to "break" the banker "in two" and a general riot broke out in the bank! Pa made quite a scene wringin' the banker's neck and would have done worse if the bank personnel hadn't held Pa back while the banker glued himself firmly under his big desk. Pa retired from the scene with vengeance in his heart. The battle was lost, but not the war by a damned sight!

The word was passed along, and when it came time for the round-up there was an unusually large contingent of weatherbeaten cowboys who volunteered to help trail the cattle to the nearest shipping point. The bank examiners went along for the ride, but the terrible clouds of dust in their nostrils, the heat, and the merciless sun added to all the other miseries, forced them to ride at the head of the bunch to get any breeze that might come up. As the long serpentine cavalcade progressed down Indian Creek, the slow-moving exhausted cattle and the weary cowpunchers stretched for miles. The examiners who were there to protect the interests of the bank, lost their alertness worrying over saddle sores, thirst and choking dust. The grinning cowboys at the end of the bunch were in worse discomfort riding into clouds of dust, forced to travel three times as far as the boys up ahead, because the fellas behind had to ride back and forth to keep calves moving along. But they'd had worse things to cope with, and the little scheme Pa had cooked up kept them snortin' with suppressed amusement as they diligently cut off bunches of cows at every opportunity. They'd drop into a draw with twenty head and come out with ten, go around a bluff with fifty and maybe not come out with any! It is safe to say, that for the failure to live up to his word, for not paying the modest share of the summer lease, the banker took a lickin' that even in those times would have amounted to thousands of dollars. Pa managed to get ahold of $800 and when the cattle were sold, he bought enough of them to obtain the brand. One of Mr. Bergman's relatives took them over, and eventually paid Pa back, starting one of the biggest herds in the country. Nothing like accumulating critters that already have your brand on 'em!

ROPIN' AN AEROPLANE

In 1905 most people in South Dakota believed the heavens were only fit for angels and birds but by 1908 the Wright brothers demonstrated their improved aeroplane to the U.S. Government. Overnight it created an unimaginable sensation. Politicians predicted that aeroplanes would completely revolutionize the "art of war" and every major country in the world began experimentation toward that end. The first aeroplane Pa ever saw, and anybody else in South Dakota for that matter, was at the 1911 Rapid City Stockmen's Meeting. A couple of the big-wigs in town, led by Fred Knockenmuss, the appointed chairman of the celebration committee and Mayor Robinson thought they'd show the cowboys and old-timers the wonders of an aeroplane flight. According to the mayor's brother, who had spent his last cent buying the contraption, this machine was going to raise itself like a bird right up into the air, soar like an eagle and land right back where it started from, in front of the cheering crowd. It was going to be a spectacular show. In fact, the committee arranged to pay the mayor's brother fifteen hundred dollars each for two flights during the week's celebrations.

When Pa heard they were going to ship the aeroplane in by rail and pay the mayor's brother such an outrageous fee, he nearly fell off his horse! First of all, didn't everybody know it always rained during the Stockmen's meeting? And why the hell didn't the damn thing fly in, if it could fly at all? Pa was Grand Marshal of the meeting and he told the Mayor and other officials the scheme was suicidal but no one listened. No sir, aviation was definitely the latest word in scientific achievement and Rapid City couldn't wait to see it!

Finally, Robinson's flying machine arrived by train and was unloaded at the depot. Pa rode over to take a look at this fly that was goin' to soar like an eagle. God Almighty! It looked like a bunch of sticks glued together with three little wheels on the bottom. If a man pushed down on one "wing" the other "wing" rose up, and it had to be tied down in case the wind blew it away! Now if that wasn't a foolish waste of three thousand dollars, Pa never saw it. Of course, the weather was already lookin' bad, as usual. Pa shook his head and rode off.

Creston Wildcats—19 _ _ 1. Pete Lemley; 2. Al Wentzer; 3. Tom Dunn; 4. Bob Lees; 5. J. Roberts; 6. R. Larsen; 7. F. Larsen; 8. Art Lees; 9. Engle; 10. Swanson; 11. Lane; 12. Brown; _ _ William _ Lemley, Sr.

The day of the wonderful flying contraption arrived and the whole town turned out for it. The ladies came in their big white hats and the men wore suits and round, black derbys. Pa never went to church, in fact he always said, "If you see somebody packin' a Bible, run like hell!" He wasn't about to dress up just to see three thousand dollars flop on its back and die. He never dressed up anyway like some cowboys did with jinglin' pointy spurs, and white wooly chaps. A man could hardly walk with all that stuff on, let alone ride a horse.

It started to drizzle a bit, just like Pa said it would, but that didn't dampen the crowd any. They'd come to see the show close up and spirits were high. The high school band played John Philip Sousa's "Stars and Stripes Forever" when Robinson came out like a knight of the round table, swash bucklin' around, bowing to the ladies, showing off like a peacock. Earlier that morning in the Stockmen's parade down Main Street Pa looked up at the cloudy sky and sure enough, the wind had picked up.

Of course, Pa never got off his horse. He just sat there smoking his pipe, waitin' for Robinson to get on with it. The mayor was all puffed out, shaking hands and smokin' a big cigar. What a great day folks! The Stockmen's Association presents ROBINSON'S AEROPLANE! After a few sputters the machine started off, it gave a little lurch, gained speed, faster still, up, up, all the men took their hats off and cheered, its up, yes, wait, its, its. . .whoops!

Pa knuckled up his mustache. An embarrassed silence fell over the crowd that just a moment before had been jumping and screaming with excitement. The drizzle turned into a warm light rain. Suddenly, a loud whoop! startled the ladies as Pa galloped past the grandstand, spun out his rope, lassoed the small back wheels of the ROBINSON AEROPLANE and pulled it out of the rocks. He dragged the injured fly back past the Mayor standing on the grandstand; the odiferous cigar now hanging from his mouth; past the amused cowboys leaning on their saddles, until he got back in front of the hushed crowd, where he left the nose-crunched machine with Aviator Robinson still hunkered down in the cockpit. Pa gallantly tipped his hat to the ladies and rode home in the rain. They tried it again a couple of days later and Pa had to rope the scientific marvel and drag it back again. He made a few bucks on that last wet duck.

The sinking of the Titanic in 1912 was nothing in comparison to the sinking of $100 income tax Pa had to fork over in 1913! People could take fool rides on boats that hit icebergs and it was their own damn fault, serves em' right, but when a man had to reach into his pocket and pull out $100 of hard-earned cash (that he wouldn't even give to his own mother) and turn around and give it to the government. . .well Pa kicked like a steer! The letter came in the mail, not long after the 16th Amendment removed the restriction that income tax be levied in proportion to state population. You could ride for miles and miles without seein' a single soul, Pa ranted, why the hell did he have to pay income tax way out on the prairie? Damn politicians, he'd like to get ahold of President

Frank Hart riding "Black Andy". Pete Lemley (Marshal of the Day) on

Taft and wring his neck! From then on, Pa was hell on lawmakers. Later, he glossed over that year of fury remembering he, "pretty near had a fit!" That was putting it mildly; 1913 was hell on Mama and the boys as well, especially after she'd just lost her generous and kindly father, Plummer Davis.

In the face of a fire spittin' husband and two little boys, one born with a hernia so that she had to make sure he never cried or exerted himself, and twenty men to cook and wash for, Mama knew there had to be some changes.

Another good dinner set the stage. Mama put on a bright clean, apron, smoothed back her shiny hair and approached Pa very gently after his stomach was full and he was havin' a smoke on his pipe. She asked Pa if now with two children they couldn't have a regular house to live in. Besides, it would be a good business investment in the long run. She probably didn't realize that she was resorting to manipulation, just as thousands of her sex were forced to do throughout the ages to improve their lives. The new house was just the distraction Pa needed to take his mind off taxes and politicians.

Pa built a nice big five-bedroom house, (for himself) with a wide front porch

Courtesy William R. Lemley, Sr.

grey horse in foreground—1905.

and a distinctive, diamond-shaped window on the stair landing. Of course, Mama never spent $800 for curtains, but the new home was a splendid mansion compared to the vermin-infested, 12x25 log cabin she had survived hell and high water to live in. Mama didn't even mind when Pa pulled the old log cabin up behind the house to use it for a bunkhouse. Every time she felt a little sad, all she had to do was look out back at that old chinked log cabin with the axed windows she had forced the hired men to make—a gentle reminder that times could be worse; she could still be living in it.

She worked hard making money to decorate her new home and before long there were handmade lace curtains and bright rugs in the kitchen, the parlor was fitted with a new rag carpet and her precious books were displayed on a bookshelf inherited from her father. Now that she had a nice home, Mama wanted to entertain, to find another way of neighboring on the isolated ranch. Except for an infrequent relative, Pa never had guests unless he was going to make money on them. Mama had to ask permission to have guests and permission was only granted if she herself paid for food and refreshments from her fancywork or chicken money. The old fancywork club needed revitalizing. How

The new house — 1907.

pleasant if the club could meet more often, she explained to Pa. She was certain that while in the company of other ladies sewing would be more enjoyable. Pete didn't like the idea but since he would benefit from the sewing club with new shirts, permission was granted. What he didn't know was that Mama had named the new club "The Ladies Mutual Improvement Club."

One hundred and fifty women came to the first meeting and about fifty came regularly thereafter. Not only did they make beautiful layers of lace, filigreed bracelets, and beribboned masterpieces of "ladies art," they wove tapestried chairs, made the tiniest beaded handbags, restored flags, and made cutwork-edged voile curtain panels, and bedspreads. So fierce was their affection for decorating their drab lives, that women indulged in a passion for lace camisoles and lovely nightgowns, anything to make themselves and their friends look and feel beautiful. They made little velvet covered boxes, hand painted scarves, and lace handkerchiefs. The gentle art of making doll clothes inspired by the richness of fairy lore, produced replicas of kings and queens, princesses and brides, cherished Christmas presents for beloved daughters. Valentine's day brought forth homemade valentines cloaked with messages and symbols: red rose for passion, white rose for purity, yellow for jealousy, lavender, mistrust. Honeysuckle meant devotion, a spider's web, good luck, a fish, fertility and good heavens, a pinecone for virginity! After the meetings, Mama led a happy sing-a-long, "Skip-To-My-Lou" and "We'll All Go Down To Rowser," At every meeting interesting reports and lectures on educational topics such as Women's Rights and Child Labor Laws created much conversation between stitches.

By 1915, Mama figured out several ways to make more money of her own. She couldn't do all the work alone:

> *I can't stand much hard work—my back gets such a crick, but
> sometimes have to do it anyway. . .Life is bad enough if we stay
> well. . .we butchered six hogs and I had to make twenty-two gallons
> of lard, and seventy pounds of sausage. There has to be a sack of
> flour cooked each week and everything else in proportion. . .for a
> week I've been sawing up wood, have many cords piled up. We
> probably won't have more than 8 or 10 boys, as Pete is gone so
> much and we don't have many neighbors. . .Pete is away a good
> deal buying war horses. Too bad to send all the best horses to be
> killed in war.*

Early in 1916 Mama realized she was pregnant. Her health was poor and she wondered how she would do all the chores, take care of the family and the cooking for hired men, the laundry, and make money besides. Her prayers were answered when Pa started the first telephone company in the area, with the switchboard located in the house, one hundred lines and twenty-five people to a line. Mother was to be the telephone operator and pay the hired woman from her wages. For once, Pa had no objections, besides, it kept his wife glued to the house and gave him more freedom. He ran for sheriff twice and lost, which made him rather hard to live with again. Ma wrote Libby that she was somewhat relieved when Pa lost: "The saloons sure worked against Pete for Sheriff as he never gives them any money. He was again defeated so I don't have to live in the jail with my boys."

WAR MEANT MONEY

Pa loved money. Only the poor think war is hell, the rich man just gets richer. World War I caused greater destruction and involved more countries than any other war up to that time. War factories cranked out newly invented weapons capable of tremendous bloodshed, larger armies were raised and extreme patriotism gave men the world over a cause they were willing to die for.

The assassination of an unknown Austrian-Hungarian Archduke Francis Ferdinand in 1914 was blamed for startin' the war but any fool knows male European pride, old feuds, and land greed started that war and every war since. Of the ten million troops killed and twenty-one million wounded in four years of awful slaughter, thousands went to their gory deaths ridin' Pete Lemley's war horses! Yes sir, war meant money.

War meant selling horses for an amazing profit. In 1915, Pa had thousands of dollars tied up in war horses which only cost him $25 per day to feed. The more Germans the better! Bring on the dirty rotten Huns! To hell with beating back the Germans with Liberty Bonds, beat them back with war horses! During World War I Pa sold six hundred and twenty-five horses in one sale alone. He got $157 for a cavalry horse, $187 for an artillery horse and $212 for a heavy artillery horse.

A girl joined the Lemley household during the war, the baby girl Mama always wanted, flaxen-haired Margaret. Pa always said, "Mama wanted a gentle girl, but sissy turned out the roughest one of the lot!" Mother sent her oldest boy Ray to Oregon to board with Aunt Libby because Pa said he didn't want Ray "cattin' around." That should have given Mama a hint of the evil to come but innocence protected her from all manner of sordid circumstances. Mama didn't want her children to live in ignorance and Ray was already showing traits of gifted intelligence. Pa thought school and books were a complete waste of time and wouldn't spend a dime on school for any of his children. It was Mama's telephone job, fancywork, butter, chickens, and later teaching jobs that put her children through high school and college. At the same time, she managed to pay

Maggie - 1918.

Ray Lemley.

hired girls, who somehow mysteriously came and went as fast as she could find them. "They are all so dirty and lazy," she told Libby, "and they cost $5.00 a week. It is with a new girl like getting a new hat. I always think how nice I will look when I get a new hat, but after I get it home, I see different." She wrote to Ray once a week with the usual motherly reminders, "If you don't have good sense about taking care of yourself, education won't count as you may get to be an educated corpse some day."

Along about this time a neighbor, Sam Barber, lost his two year-old son. The sweet little child wandered away and drowned in Rapid Creek. Pa and the other men searched the flooded stream for hours until they finally found the body a mile downstream. The handsome boy had light golden ringlets and Mama took the lifeless child and tried to clean him up before it broke his mother's heart to see him. She washed his hair and combed it and the naturally curly ringlets formed again on his forehead and behind his ears. Mama never knew then she would someday lose her own golden haired boy to the dangerous natural elements on the South Dakota prairie.

Pa was buying horses anywhere he could find them. A rancher he knew had a beautiful bay team and Pa was bound to have them. He offered to buy the horses for a great deal of money but the man said he wouldn't part with the team for anything. Pa then tried to trade with horses that were worth more money but again the rancher said no. One day Pa discovered some of his cows bawlin' in the pasture. Their calves were missing and Pa knew he'd been the victim of a rustler. He and one of his hired men started searching for the calves, fanning out in a circle both ways. They made wider circles, listening for bawlin' calves who undoubtedly were missing their mothers. On the third day, the hired man discovered a barn on a neighbor's place with a load of bawlin' calves. He and Pa rounded up the mother cows and took them over. When the calves saw their mothers they immediately began to suck and the bawlin' stopped.

Pa rode up to the ranch house and called the man to come out! It just happened to be the man who owned the beautiful bay team of horses Pa coveted. The rancher's son came out and Pa told him that he wouldn't call the Sheriff if the rancher would make out a bill of sale for the bay team and bring it out damn quick! The boy went back into the house and for a long time nothing happened. Finally, Pa rode up in front of the house and yelled that he was goin' for the Sheriff. Just then the boy came out and handed Pa the bill of sale. "He didn't want to part with his bay team but he parted with them alright!" Pa gloated. Several days later, the man's haystacks all burnt up and they never caught the rascal who did it.

They didn't ever catch the rascal who caused so much havoc in the little town of New Underwood, either. Seems somebody found out there was to be an exhibition of two lady wrestlers and the whole town came out to see the outrageous sight. The women wore bright-colored tights and looked altogether scandalous rollin' around on the mat, sweatin' and cussin'. Pa went to see the "ladies" and he said somebody must have put hot itchy powder on the wrestlin' mat because when the "ladies" got to sweatin' and rollin' they jumped up and went to scratchin' like mad. Pa laughed and thought it was hilarious the "ladies" felt like they'd been, "bit like fire." He had escaped from the scene of the crime in his first car.

Probably after years of ignoring Mother's quiet advice to purchase an automobile, Pa finally decided he'd made enough money selling war horses to buy himself a classy Essex Convertible. Mama might have had second thoughts once Pa got behind the wheel! If he was a daredevil on a horse, he was just as adventurous in a car, in fact nobody was safe for miles around when Pa got into his car, especially the auto itself.

Once he got the car home, one of the first places he went was on a rabbit hunt, but this was no ordinary rabbit hunt. Mama waved from the porch as Pa and some neighbors left on the grand hunt, Pa distinguished in his beaver coat, a cigar stickin' out of the side of his mouth, and his rifle across the steerin' wheel just like a saddle horn. Mama didn't go because she never liked to kill an animal of any kind, not even a chicken, unless she had to. But oh, that Essex was a beautiful sight as it pulled out of the yard. Pa even bought himself the latest automobile cap to go with it, the first time Mama had ever seen him without a 13X Beaver Stetson of the finest grade.

To prepare for the hunting trip she had polished the elegant brown leather upholstery, and shined the brass knobs and narrow front window until they gleamed. There wasn't a speck of dirt on that car when she finished, not even on the wheels. That afternoon when she heard the chugging car motor, she ran out to greet the hunters returning from the illustrious chase. It certainly must have been a chase alright. There was Pa, proud as a peacock with the Essex convertible piled over five feet high with a hundred bloody rabbits, fur, ears, and rabbit's feet sticking out of every crevice of the car! From that moment on, Mama knew that poor automobile was going to have a hard time of it. The brakes didn't last six months and whenever Pa wanted to stop the car he headed for the nearest corner post and hollered, "Whoa! Whoooa!"

As all good things must come to an end, so did the war. Pa and Henry McCain took their financial lives in their hands and bought a big bunch of horses from all over the country to sell to the Allies. It was on one of those horse buyin' trips that Pa wrote out a check for horses on a piece of bark, and what was even more precarious, on an account which didn't even begin to have that much money in it. Amazingly, the banker honored the check and put enough money in Pa's account to cover it. Hundreds of thousands of dollars and neither Pa nor his friend could have made that much money in twenty years. McCain was an upstanding young man who shared his wife's fanatical aversion to liquor of any kind. On November 11, 1918, Pa and Henry McCain were visited by representatives from France and Britain who had arrived to buy all of the horses they had.

Earlier that morning, Pa rode over to New Underwood, about nineteen miles east of Rapid City, intending to get the mail and a few groceries. To his conster-

The Rabbit Hunt—1916.

nation he found out the Armistice had been signed and the war was over! This was real trouble and certain ruin if all those horses couldn't be sold. He bought the groceries and all the jugs of whiskey he could carry on the horse and headed for home.

Nothing at all was said to the European visitors about the wonderful news. McCain, who hated the taste of liquor, had a broken leg and had to stay in the house with the Frenchman and drink whiskey. The yawning pits of hell for the drunkard was preferable to a lifetime of slavery trying to pay off the bank! One step away from his horse was too far to walk according to Pa. But that day he ran out into the fields in his cowboy boots, jumping and crawlin' around helping the Englishman catch butterfly specimens for his collection. Swish! Swish! The butterfly net swished past McCain who was looking out the window. He nearly blew the whole show when he saw Pa out in the pasture. He was so drunk he just got down on his broken leg and howled with laughter, tears streamin' down his face. Just then, Pa jumped like a ballerina past the window into the air and McCain fell backwards on the floor and wet his pants. Pa glared through the window at him. This lasted all day long. As soon as the "furriners" selected their horses and the money was in Pa's butterfly-dusted hands, the visitors departed. McCain was sick for a week, but he didn't know whether he was goin' to die from the liquor or kill himself laughin'. Later Pa explained how he'd always conducted his business. With the usual honest sincerity and patriotic conviction in his voice he said, "Hell, it didn't mean a damn thing to those governments, and it would have ruined us for life!"

Maggie Lemley—1920.

SAVING GRACE

Pa always knew a storm was coming when the sun came up pink and navy blue over Rattlesnake Butte. He hated the white fluff he called "poison snow," because it meant everyone had to work that much harder, feeding animals, keeping watch over cattle and horses in temperatures that fell to fifty degrees below zero and more.

Winters were hardest on Mother, whose health had grown progressively worse. She was still having a difficult time keeping hired girls, a month or so went by, she'd wake up one morning and another girl had vanished into the night. No one was kinder to hired help than Mama, considerate and gentle with cooking and chore supervision. It seemed strange to lose one hired woman after another. In 1919, she was cooking for fourteen and doing the heavy chores herself. "What in the dickens can I cook for ten men these, wheatless, meatless, eat-less times," she wrote Libby. Pa was traveling, first as head judge for the Belle Fourche Tri-State Round-up (rodeo) and then off to Nevada for the exciting Jack Dempsey-Jess Willard boxing match. Mama stayed home. When Ray graduated from High School Pa wouldn't take her, though she'd paid all Ray's expenses and wanted so to be there.

When the 1918 influenza epidemic killed thousands of Americans and brought the country to its knees, everyone in the family got it. Mother nursed one after another back to health. She was having trouble breathing, but nobody noticed. It was along about this time when new neighbors moved on land adjoining the ranch and Ma was pleased because the new family had a little daughter the same age as Margaret. Pa was not pleased; the new neighbors were sheepherders!

Ranchers called sheep "hoofed locusts, stinkers, stubble jumpers, maggots, and baa-aahs." The competition for remaining public domain was fierce among cattle ranchers, homesteaders, and sheepmen. Sheep raisers saw faster profits, grazed sheep on range that wouldn't support cattle, needed less water, and suffered fewer losses. On top of that, sheepherders had year-round jobs and two products to sell, wool and mutton. Once sheep got into a cattleman's pasture, they ate it bare:

Ezekiel (34:18.) It is a small thing to you, O evil shepherds, that you not only keep the best of the pastures for yourselves, but trample down the rest?

Violence erupted in Texas and Colorado leaving fifty dead men and the slaughter of at least 53,000 sheep. Ranchers disdained men who herded on foot with dogs, men they called "mutton punchers, lamb lickers, and snoozers." In a little known act of violence, thirty-two South Dakota cattlemen killed a sheepherder and all his sheep and as an afterthought, paid his widow $1,000 in silver to get out.

Pa called sheepherders "scabs." The neighboring scab had two teenage boys as well as a girl. They were like flies, an annoyance to Pa. It wasn't long before they gained quite a reputation for bootleggin' and that's how they survived as long as they did. One particular still was found in a clump of bushes with the smokestack sticking up and telltale smoke drifting from it. There was no tellin' how many people for miles around got their "Sheep Mountain Dew" from the scab.

One day the sheepherder and his boys went down on Rapid Creek and proceeded to cut down a tree to get at a beehive hanging from a top branch. The tree was on Pa's land and he and one of his hired men happened to be nearby. Pa stormed up and yelled, "Get the hell off my land you damned scabs!" The hired man rode up to the sheepherder and butted him with the horse. "You stay out of this!" the scab growled. The hired man paid no attention and kept comin'. The lamb-licker grabbed his rifle off the wagon and shot the horse dead! A beautiful buckskin crumpled to the ground, its powerful head fell limp to one side. In disbelief, Pa's cowpuncher bent over the body of the horse. In a few split seconds Pa made a decision that affected the rest of his life. Although the scab had killed one of his favorite mounts, a horse he had broken and trained, and the hired man was crushed and blubbering, Pa wasn't hit in his heart, he was hit in the wallet, a much deadlier place. The scab would pay and pay dearly, but with so many witnesses, he wouldn't pay that day. Pa pulled his hired man up behind him and galloped off.

In mid-April 1920 Pa found sheep in one of his pastures and beat them off. The young scabbie was herdin' at the time and he pulled out his rifle. Pa grabbed the gun from the kid's hands and broke it over a rock. Of course, the boy ran to his dad and told the old snoozer what had happened. The scabbie was given another gun and told to use it if Pete Lemley came near the sheep again. Sure enough, on April 28th the lazy boy was out herdin', sat down under a tree, and forgot about his sheep. The stubble jumpers wandered into Pa's pasture and were busy destroying it when he rode up. The kid was flat on his back holdin' up a western magazine, paying no attention at all to his business when Pa started beating the maggots back. Ten year-old Chauncey rode alongside Pa. This time, the scabbie had a 32 rifle with him and before Chauncey or Pa could do anything, the boy shot at them, narrowly missing the back of Chauncey's head. Pa pulled out his pistol and shot the boy's hat off, thinking it would scare him off. Having been in Buffalo Bill's Wild West, he was a crack shot with any type of gun. One quick shot was all Pa needed to nail the kid but he was just a boy and besides, Chauncey was with him. Just then, a bullet glanced off Pa's collar button and went deep into his shoulder. The scabbie quickly used up all his ammunition and Pa rode up to him and drew a bead straight down into his eyes. The boy took off runnin'. When he got home he must have fabricated a good tale because the next day the Rapid City Journal carried a front page article about the "gunfight" that all the Lemleys sure got a kick out of:

> *There had been no arrests made last night and it was impossible to verify the reports that were current on the street yesterday. According to the reports the fight was with six shooters – Lemley being hit twice in the arm before exhausting his ammunition when he threw up his hands and called to the boy to stop. It is said the boy got a bullet hole through his hat. Reports agree that there has been bad blood between the two families for some time.*

Pa wasn't about to kill a young kid in front of his own son but it might have been different if the old scab had been around. No doctor was called to remove the bullet; it stayed in his shoulder the rest of his life, just like the one next to his heart.

The scabs drank too much and Mama didn't want her children shot at accidentally or on purpose. She had to go to Rapid City to have some teeth pulled but she was uncomfortable about leaving the children. Pa kept a close eye on his pastures, and a wrong move on the part of Mr. Scab was going to be his last one. Later on, after years of hard feelings, the scabs finally lost their ranch to drought and poor management. Pa got ahold of their property with great and lasting satisfaction.

As time went on, Mama's toothache finally became unbearable so Pa took Mother to Rapid City and the children went along. It was just going to be an overnight stay. Little Maggie was four years old, quick and as wild as a March hare. Chauncey was a lot like Pa, looked like him and acted like him, except he had a funny, wonderful disposition. He was the best cowboy of the three children and Pa's constant criticism didn't dampen his spirits one bit. Pa blamed Chauncey for everything and he didn't deserve it; everybody knew Chauncey was Pa's whipping boy. The good natured brother called his little sister "Gabe," short for Gabriel the angel. He protected and watched out for her whenever he wasn't overworking long hours in the saddle with no pay.

Pullin' teeth was damn serious business. Mama went under ether and was placed in a recovery room nearby. Everything went fine until the nurse forgot to check in on her. Unconscious, her mouth open and gasping for the breath that would not come, Mama's frail limbs contorted with violent chills and foam bubbled out of her mouth. The nurse felt quickly for a pulse but the racing heart beat and ghastly white skin told the tale. For the next three weeks pneumonia tried to kill Grace Lemley. She went in and out of consciousness, her hair fell out from the top of her head in great clumps, and the doctors gave up hope. Ray was called home from college and Grandma Davis prepared the grandchildren for their mother's coming death, washed and pressed their best clothes, and the house was cleaned for the expected visitors after the funeral. Mama was going to die.

Doctors were not Pa's favorite people. He absolutely hated hospitals and anything that looked or smelled like needles. He hadn't once been to see Mama, claiming he was too busy at the ranch. When it finally looked to him that she wasn't goin' to make it, he went alone to Rapid City. The Essex plowed into the curb in front of the hospital, Pa's usual method of stopping a car that had no brakes, and he walked up the wide steps to the door. How he hated to walk anyplace, let alone into a damn death house! When he got to her room he stood in the doorway and glared at his wife. Mama was semi-conscious. Every once in awhile she'd groan, an incoherent babble, a sudden jerking movement and then she was still. He stood looking down at her. God, she looked like hell. "Grace! Grace!" From somewhere deep inside her brain, Mama heard Pa call her name. He took ahold of her arm and shook her, "Here, you come back here Grace Lemley, do you hear me?" he demanded. "I'm not puttin' up with any of this!" Grace remembered she was about ready to go off into a happy, friendly place when Pa shook her. She was so used to minding him, so afraid of displeasing him, she decided she'd better not die.

I had to stay in the hospital six weeks. Three weeks are just a blank to me. My hair all came out as well as my teeth, and I am still weak. I think they put me in a cold room while unconscious. . .and didn't take care of me right. The whole family could have wintered at Long Beach for my expenses, as had to have a day and a night nurse for three weeks and one all the time. I don't think so much of doctors as I did, but maybe our tribe will produce a better quality than now litters the earth. Pete told me I had to get well and I said I would.

Nearly two months after they first took her to the hospital, the family watched in horror as Mama cut off forty-five inch braids of thin, wispy hair. She saw their long faces and told them bobbed hair was in style. Maggie held up the long headless braids to Pa when he came to take Mama home and he backed up like he'd been shot.

Comin' home Mother sensed something strange, something different, as they pulled into the winding road that led to the ranch, past the same swimmin' hole in the frozen creek, the bare apple trees, the sleeping lilac bushes heavy with snow.

Pa went to the barn and Ray carried his mother through the gate to the back kitchen door, nearly stumbling in the darkness. "Be careful, don't drop her!" Chauncey scolded. "Let me carry her in!" The snow crunched under their feet as they scrambled to find the doorlatch. Little Maggie tugged at the quilt Ray had carefully wrapped around his thin, gaunt mother, "Mama's home, Mama's home," she sang. Oh, how nice to smell the old familiar kitchen. "Chauncey, light the lamp, will you dear?" Mama asked weakly. Chauncey giggled, "You bet I will, Mama!"

Suddenly, the kitchen glowed in a brilliant light! The children squealed, Maggie jumped up and down, and Mama blinked . . .and blinked again. While Mother lay dying in the hospital, Pa installed electricity in the house and even into the 10x12 laundry shed — a Delcro Electricity system — the first in the area. And the laundry shed had a new round, wringer washing machine in it.

Whether the expectation of her death or pure guilt had driven Pa to give his wife the second gift of their twenty-three years of marriage, Mama never knew. For a woman who had believed in all the promises of married life, enough to work herself to death for them, it was enough just to be alive and home at last. But as she was carried from one well-lit room to another, Mama must have realized that life would never be quite the same again.

Maggie and friend—1921

WHEN RATTLESNAKES ARE BLIND

"Whatta my bid, ladies and gentlemen? Whatta my bid?" Chauncey mimiced Pa the auctioneer. "Do I hear five dollars? Thank you sir, do I hear five thousand?" Maggie laughed till she cried. Chauncey was a miniature Will Rogers, entertaining little sister with funny antics that kept her occupied for hours and it wasn't easy. The golden hair had to be kept short because she was into every kind of mischief. Quick as lightning, (perhaps even a fox), she was happiest when she wriggled free from shoes and ran barefoot through the yard where Ray kept his baby rattlesnakes. Fearless, she jumped over one, then another, squealing with delight each time one tried to bite. She idolized Chauncey and kept him busy rescuing his tiny sister "Gabe" from untold predicaments. One day the neighbor's cat died and Chauncey decided Maggie should attend a proper funeral. Since the unfortunate feline was a "Catholic cat," he should have a proper Catholic burial. Chauncey draped a dish-towel and a black slicker over himself and gave a good imitation of the Latin rites, much to the amusement of the owner who was hiding behind the shed. Another time he let one of the cats lick the hired man's whiskey and took him home to Mama. She was hanging up clothes when she caught sight of the in-ebriated animal. "Chauncey! What in the world is the matter with that cat!" For a few minutes Mama thought the cat might be rabid and her heart skipped a beat. But she soon caught on to Chauncey's joke and had a serious talk with him about hurting a defenseless animal. She was patient with her children, taking time to listen while a boy told long stories or a little girl asked endless questions. On the other hand, Pa didn't pay a bit of attention to them until they were old enough to work. By that time they were all voracious readers and had to hide their books from Pa, who hated what he considered a fool's pastime. In the summertime Chauncey built sand castles for "Gabe" on Rapid Creek and mended Pa's har-ness after he caught Maggie cutting it up to make harnesses for her dog. Chauncey opened the barn door and there she sat in a pile of ruined rivets, "Jeez, Gabe, you're goin' to catch it!"

Ray went off to Macalester College in St. Paul and Mama knew she had to pay the expensive tuition if her son were to fulfill his dream of becoming a

Chauncey Lemley with his rabbits—1921.

doctor. Mother's Peabody breeding instilled her with a love of education, of books, artwork, the finer things in life, yet she lived in a constant state of insecurity, saving every penny, selling fancywork, eggs, and butter, the telephone switchboard job, making muscrat muffs, sewing, anything to put books in her children's hands and shoes on their feet. Summers the kids ran off to the hayloft to read, hiding precious volumes where Pa wouldn't find them in cozy nests under loose floorboards, or in the secret bookcase in Mama's dry cellar. It wasn't as easy during the winter when the only warm place to read was next to the kitchen stove. If Pa saw a child over eight, he found a hard job for him or her to do and it took a load of craftiness to stay out of his way.

Meanwhile, the world was changing for women. On June 4, 1919 Congress passed the 19th Amendment to the Constitution and while Mother was recuperatin' from her brush with death, the amendment was ratified. She had time to read what the world was saying about the gentler sex:

There is something trim and trig and confident about her. She is easy in her manners. There is music in her laugh. She is youth, she is hope, she is romance—she is wisdom!
H.L. Mencken, Editor, Smart Set

I believe in woman's suffrage wherever the women want it.
Theodore Roosevelt

By 1920 more than eight million American women held gainful occupations. Gone were the tight corsets, pinched so tight that breathin' was difficult, skirts were mid-calf, up and out of the mud at last. Suffragists Elizabeth Cady Stanton and Susan B. Anthony didn't live long enough to hear a shout for joy when twenty-six million newly enfranchised women got the vote, but from her sick-bed Mama heard the distant sounds of gleeful laughter.

One spring morning in 1922, Pa heard the Essex start up. He thought it was the hired man and he forgot about it. The next morning and the next he heard the motor again. The man must be working on the car, Pa reckoned; he sure never worked on it himself; wouldn't even take the time to oil it, hell no, another waste of time. Pa was out in the corral closing the gate when out of the barn came the Essex, horn tootin' and chickens squawkin' to get out of the way! Pa's eyes widened, his mouth dropped open, and he leaped aside just as Grace Josephine Lemley drove past, laughing and wavin' her hat in the air. Pa looked around for his pipe as Mama pulled onto the road in a cloud of dust, still wavin' her veiled traveling hat, long pink streamers flyin' in the wind. At the age of forty-one, suffering from emphysema and heart problems, Mama was goin' off to college! Determined to provide the education for her children that Pa disdained, she drove herself to college classes in Spearfish and earned a teaching certificate.

That fall Mother taught school, seventy-five dollars a month teaching eight

us Maggie caught in the act.

grades in a run down claim shack. One of her happiest and naughtiest pupils, Maggie Lemley, beamed to think Mama had saved her from liftin' heavy hay bales in order to learn from the books she had grown to cherish. It was a country school, a dilapitated old building that Pa, as head of the School Board, refused to fix up. Early in the morning, cold and snowy or pouring rain, Mama pulled Maggie up on "Shorty," a truly phlegmatic old horse, and with Chauncey running along beside to get him goin', they trotted down the road, a long three miles to school through blizzards and all the terrors a South Dakota winter can hold. Maggie helped the teacher sweep out the building every morning and built the fire. Children filed in and teacher started out the day with a song on the harmonica. Strains of "Old Dog Tray" or "Tenting Tonight On the Old Campground," "Juanita" and "Home Sweet Home" could be heard coming from that happy little shack on the hill, a trail of woodsmoke rising from the chimney into the frosty air. Long before people heard of "winding down" Mama used this technique with her students, reading a chapter twice a day from their favorite books. The pupils sat wide-eyed as she read a book by Albert Payson Terhune, O. Henry, or Horatio Alger. They all cried buckets of tears over Jack London's Call Of The Wild, and they strained with the hero "Buck" to pull a thousand pounds for his adored master. The children listened with bated breath to James Oliver Curwood's exciting novels and were inspired by books which stressed Mama's feminine ideals of loyalty, honesty, and faithfulness.

Teacher was always careful of childrens' feelings and pride was held sacred. If she thought a child's lunch pail wasn't full enough, she never said a thing. Gingersnap cookies and cocoa appeared early in the afternoon and whether hungry or not, Maggie ate whatever was offered right along with the rest. The hungry child never suspected the nourishing milk and cookies were just for him. When a boy's jacket needed mending, out came a tiny sewing basket while the children were at recess.

Maggie found out that teacher mended on occasion when she had to stay in for recess for some minor infraction of the rules, like the time she brought baby rattlesnakes to drop in the outhouse toilets, which certainly got a rise out of everyone in the midst of very serious business activities. Or the spring morning she dipped her snobby blond classmate's braid into the ink well. And of course, there was the most exciting day of the year, April 1, 1927, when Effie Tweeter surprised the long squirmy centipede nestled comfortably in one of her best white gloves! Lovely spiders with black silken bodies, soft skunks, sharp-clawed baby bats and other sweet creatures of the fields and streams always had a way of showing up in Maggie's vicinity even though Ma carefully frisked her innocent daughter every morning before school. Whenever one of the poor critters found its way into someone's lunchpail or coat pocket, teacher took the opportunity to discuss the scientific nature and habits of each and every one. At the end of the year students knew quite a lot about wild animal behavior, often much more than they ever cared to know.

Maggie and Mama – 1921.

Mrs. Lemley's philosophy of making a warm, interesting, song-filled day at school a lot more inviting than pitchin' hay or haulin' water, sent many a country child deep into the glorious and fantastic adventures of a good book and later into science, business, and legal careers. One semester a student brought a tiny four year-old to visit school. He was considered something of a little genius and later proved a whiz at inventing things. Stanley was very well behaved, as all the other children were, with the exception of Maggie, and after the teacher had the other children lined up with work, she approached Stanley and asked, "What would you rather do, Stanley, draw things on this tablet, or maybe look at this book of pictures?" Without changing his expression, Stanley looked down at his feet and muttered, "I'd drudder eat!"

Another time a little fellow was recitin' "Little Jack Horner," with teacher coaxing along. Beamin' triumphantly he said aloud, "stuck in his thumb, pulled out a plum, and said what a fart boy am I!" Years later that funny boy grew up into an enormous, quite homely businessman. Teacher never met him later with all his courteous manners that she didn't see that little boy with the delighted expression on his face re-designing the nursery rhyme.

School recess was always wonderful, winter or spring. Somebody harnessed a horse to a toboggan and there were lots of trees to climb. A "flying Dutchman" was erected for the childrens' amusement, a large plank mounted on a wagon axle. One child got close to the axle and pushed while the child on each end whirled around faster and faster. Mother just expected the children to have good sense and good reflexes and they rarely got into fights, with the usual exception of Maggie who took on the biggest boys with little, if any provocation.

School was such a rest from work on the ranch but even at home Mama tried to break the tediousness of hard work with an occasional surprise. She baked the most delicious cream puffs filled with sweet whipped cream, mouth-watering treats the hired men clamored for after supper. One night the men headed in for the evening meal half-starved as usual and Mama served delicious baked ham, creamy mashed potatoes, biscuits, gravy, and vegetables piping hot—a meal to melt in the mouth. They cleaned their plates, pushin' biscuits around to sponge up the gravy until there wasn't a scrap left on the table. Then it was time for dessert. Mama brought out the cream puffs on a big serving platter, and twelve men chomped down on the treats with great gusto! A sudden hush fell over the room as only one polite man continued eating, never blinking an eye. He chewed and chewed, and smiled, and chewed. A big glob filled one cheek, pretty soon he had a glob in both cheeks, but he just kept smilin' and chewin'. The mannerly old boy might have swallowed the fluffy confection if mother hadn't let him off the hook. Instead of whipped cream, the baked puffs were filled with cotton!

Ma grasped life with a more hopeful view of human nature than events sometimes warranted. Strangely enough, people just seemed to go out of their way to justify Mama's faith in their better selves. One of her failures was a hired man named Vaughn Steele. He was a black-eyed, soft-spoken, and apparently

Mama's class—1923. Maggie standing left. Chauncey with his dog

well-educated wanderer. Mother was very partial to him, in great part because of his more sophisticated sense of humor. They frequently found things funny they didn't laugh out loud about. Maggie helped Vaughn sort through the potatoes in the old cellar while he regaled her with stories of escapes from Sing Sing through the sewers and other terrible tales, sometimes a little reminiscent of *Les Miserables,* which Maggie hadn't read yet. No doubt Vaughn must have read the book well because she believed every word. Eventually, he moved on and after he left Mama found magazine margins filled with her signature, obviously practiced by Steele and perfectly done. She privately appreciated his devotion to perfection until a later conference with the bank revealed a check for $800 that was not of her making. Authorities were notified, and the bank made good on the check, and that was for all practical purposes the end of it. They rarely caught vagabond criminals in those days. About six months later Vaughn returned, just as polite, personable, and certainly brave as he always was. Mama was very nice to him, invited him to supper, and he went out to the bunkhouse to sleep and moved on the next day. No one except Mama and Maggie ever knew of his visit and they didn't tell anyone. It's strange how he knew Papa was gone just at that time. Nothing was ever said again about the forged check.

Maggie's early instincts were to "thwart the sheriff" if possible. When she was seven years old Pa hired a man named "Buck" who sat among the June pasqueflowers and whittled wondrous toys for Maggie after his daily work was finished. He whistled "Way Down Upon The Swanee River" sculpting miniature bears, rabbits, and birds that could almost fly away, piling them up in a little wooden wheelbarrow.

One afternoon the sheriff came along and hid in the shed waitin' for Buck to get home from feeding the cattle. "Mama, is the Sheriff waitin' for Pa?" Maggie asked.

"Well . . . no, not Pa," she hedged. In an instant Maggie streaked to the timber. When the hay wagons came in sight, Buck had disappeared and no one ever saw him again. Pa had a time explaining the whereabouts of his hired man, although he was probably glad he didn't have to pay the accumulated back wages. Maggie was also nowhere to be found, a typical activity—she just melted into the scenery when the going got dicey! Mama seemed to understand Maggie's little absences and never spoke to her in a harsh or condemning manner no matter how shocking the crime. If she thought Maggie needed to learn a lesson she told stories to illustrate the point she wanted to get across. One of the stories Maggie heard quite often was about two mothers with their two dressed-up girls walking down a muddy path. The one mother airily pointed out a butterfly flying in the right direction. The other mother nagged and cautioned Nellie not to get near that mud puddle, but of course Nellie fell right in.

Somewhere hidden in her mind, Mama still possessed a touch of romance. She read the latest novels as well as the classics. She played the piano and sang for hours, a great hit at the country dances, if she could get to one. With

"Pals."

Chauncey—1923.

Grace and Maggie with "Jack" and friend.

Maggie looking over her shoulder, Mama paged through Montgomery Ward catalogues, always stopping on the pages filled with diamond rings and pendants, rubbing her fingers softly over the pictures. The day came when she managed to trade an old broken-down piano for a small diamond engagement ring and never took it off again. That dream came true even though the groom had nothing to do with it. She still wrote often to Libby: "No, I haven't felt any too well since my sick spell last winter, and had to work right along. Doctor says my heart, and orders change of climate."

Though not in good health, Mother always saw to it that her kids had some fun, and what a joy the twenties were for children! Marbles were the rage and Maggie and Chauncey got to be pretty good at it. They were happily unaware that 1925 brought Calvin Coolidge his fourth year in office, but they knew every William S. Hart movie by heart. On Saturdays, if he could get away from Pa, Chauncey went to the Palace Theatre in Rapid City and Maggie tagged along listening to the teenage boys talking about Lou Gehrig and the great Babe Ruth's 39th home run in early August.

Some say August is the month when rattlesnakes are blind and dangerous and that is the month when Chauncey left home for the last time. There were few child labor laws and Pa made him work hard in rain, sleet, or shine. Chauncey was conscientious and took all Pa threw at him. Sometimes if Pa caught the boy readin', he'd grab the book, stomp on it, and then yell at him as a trumped-up excuse to send the boy on an errand. Chauncey left early in the morning to tend cattle and Pa had him workin' until dark. When the sun went down, Pa made everyone go to bed because they all had to be up at 4 a.m. Every morning started out the same way. Pa growled from bed at the hired woman (or Ma) to get up and get the fire on, he cussed and muttered and nagged until Mama could take it no longer. Nobody wanted to sleep in the room above Pa's bedroom because it was a terrible way to greet the day.

Chauncey left one morning in the drizzling rain. The weather was hot in August with swarms of biting black knats, but the days had been unusually mild. Pa made Chauncey go out in the pre-dawn hours to herd cattle alone and the boy went quietly after gulping breakfast. He was gone all day with no lunch and was late comin' in for supper, which wasn't like him. By eight in the evening, Mama knew something was terribly wrong. She sat on the front porch and rocked, listening to the rain and the hall clock strike the hour, every hour, all night long.

That night in the rain Pa and the hired men searched every ravine, ridge, and field on the ranch. They passed Chauncey's riderless horse coming home about daylight. Mama stood up from the rocker and covered her face with her apron as the horse walked slowly into the barn. Chauncey was a good cowboy, could ride better than others, and knew the ranch like the palm of his hand. The riderless horse could only mean one thing, the beloved laughing boy, the child who had taken unnecessary abuse all his life was out there somewhere alone and in trouble. After ten hours in the saddle, Pa rode up to a remote, rocky area

Chauncey three years before he died.

of the ranch with a neighbor, James Dunn. It was a dangerous place for a horse and rider, the last place in the world Chauncey would ever go. Scrunched on the rocks, his body twisted one way and his neck another, lay Chauncey Lemley. In balmy weather except for a light rain, the horse must have stumbled, throwing Chauncey against a rock so hard it killed him instantly. Pa lifted the boy he had nagged and overworked, blamed, and ridiculed, pulled him up to a sitting position and carried him home.

Mother was still on the porch, rocking slowly back and forth while Maggie played at her feet with the dog. A massive thundercloud came up suddenly in the southwest, beautiful mushroomed layers of champagne mother-of-pearl force, an awesome, pushing, pulsating power climbing higher and higher in the sky. Hushed stillness; broken only by swallows swooping in and out of the barn, darting up and diving straight down, their strange dance signaling the approach of the summer storm. Mama was looking up at the huge billowy clouds nearly straight overhead when she and Maggie heard a sound they had never heard before. Down through the pasture next to the house came a weird cry. Mother stood up suddenly and grabbed the porch railing and Maggie held her skirt tightly as the dog crept closer. Pa rode alone past the porch, his body hunched over his dead son.

He moaned and carried on for a week and Maggie hoped he was sorry for treating Chauncey the way he had. There were funeral arrangements to make, food to cook, the house to clean, the guests began to arrive. Mama threw herself into the grieving work and did all the necessary things herself, combed his hair for the last time, dressed him, choked with sorrow. She remembered Pa's cruel demands on the child, his degrading criticism when Chauncey tried to draw a picture or brought her a flower from the fields. Her own tired words when the boy came into the kitchen dripping wet from the creek holding his soaked shoes behind him. Every funny joke he told she laughed at through the tears, "Whatta my bid ladies and gentlemen? Whatta my bid?"

Before the casket lid closed forever over the beloved face of her sunny boy, she ran her hand gently over his forehead, his nose, the handsome mouth and chin. She put her head down to his face and quietly thanked God her boy was resting at last. Mama was to think of him everyday for the rest of her life, especially on the first birthday after his death, the most painful for mothers. As if he were there yet, she would turn suddenly, forgetting. Is he in out of the storm? Has he eaten breakfast yet? She kept all his little boyish treasures, hers now in a white box; his favorite cowboy belt, the leather wallet he made for himself, the ring with the red stone.

The first little red-haired baby was lost before the first spoken word, before the first toddling step. But to lose a child after fifteen years of loving and caring for him, stroking his arms at night when he got sick, laughing at his antics in the bathtub, folding and ironing his clothes; missing him tore at her heart.

On the way to Rapid City, the long funeral caravan abruptly stopped when

Chauncey, Ray, Maggie, Mama, and Pa.

the hearse had a flat tire. Maggie got out and ran around to the tire. "Oh Mama," she smiled through the tears, "Chauncey would love this! He'd think it was the funniest thing, to have a flat tire on the way to his funeral!"

Chauncey Lemley's death was viewed with suspicion by friends and relatives, cloaked in the mystery that had always surrounded Pa's life. People never accepted the accidental death story, whispering that it was probably the scabs who had murdered him, a successful vendetta, or worse, that Pa had somehow killed him, worked to death. But Pa maintained that his son had been thrown from his horse on the rain-slick rocks and his neck broken in the fall. Since it was August, Chauncey's horse might have spooked a rattlesnake and thrown him off. Pa could size up a situation quicker and better than anybody else and if he said it was an accident, it must have been an accident. If somebody had murdered Chauncey, the Nightrider would have taken care of him and that didn't happen. The only thing that really mattered was that the best little cowboy was gone.

Mama's Chevvie Coupe — late 1920s

THE "CHEVVIE" COUPE

Several years after Chauncey died Pa bought the State Bank of Scenic. Mama warned him against it but what did a woman know? "Pete, you're a great horseman and rancher but you're no banker," she warned him. He ignored her advice but she somehow ended up President of the Scenic Bank Board and had to do most of the paperwork. The Scenic banker was never reckless with his money and he made sure loans only went to men with steady incomes.

Mother wrote to Libby describing a showdown she had with the wily new banker:

Now I will tell you how I bought the car, and don't you dare laugh! The Essex was getting old and as no one fixed anything on it, I usually had a catastrophe when I went anywhere. One day I started early to Rapid for Teacher's Institute — due at 9 a.m. It took me five hours and lots of trouble. I vowed I'd trade the brute off, which I did. Got $100.00 allowance on a new one and came home in the new coupe. My husband ordered me right away to get the Essex right back here. I bought it back for $50.00 though what does he want with the old wreck?

Pa was absolutely furious! He demanded his car back and Mama had to bring it all the way back to the ranch. It was a humiliating experience but she made up her mind she was keeping the "Chevvie" and would pay for it herself! For once, there was nothing he could say. There were no brakes on the Essex, and the gears were all but gone.

Margaret and I go to Rapid for a music lesson every Saturday, and now we go in comfort. But the fun of it is now whenever he goes anywhere, he goes in the "Chevvie" as it is always ready to go. The other two wrecks just sit around. MEN NEVER GET ASHAMED OF THEMSELVES!

Maggie wheedled Pa out of $75 worth of alfalfa seed, and Ma had to pay for the Chevrolet Pa now drove.

Mama's new visions extended to real estate. She talked Pa into buying a house in Rapid City and had visions of owning more. "Rapid City is booming," she wrote Libby. "They just finished a nine story hotel and lots of building going on. One man is bound to build a garage right up against our house in town, and I'm trying to out-bid him on the lots." Pa didn't like Mama's real estate dreams so he stubbornly refused to buy any more land because he couldn't "pasture any cows on it." The lots Mama wanted to buy cost two thousand dollars, which later brought some lucky owner seventy-eight thousand dollars! In 1928, Pa rented forty thousand acres of summer pasture in the Badlands for six hundred dollars. He paid the Indians cash and he got it dirt cheap. It was the only thing that saved Pa when the bottom dropped out of the banking business in 1930. Herbert Hoover left the country in an awful fix and Franklin D. Roosevelt came into power saying he was goin' to change everything. Pa always held politicians and elected officials strictly accountable for every imaginable calamity. Roosevelt was his personal "bete noir." He voted for him the first time around, but a lot of those reforms were a bit hard to swallow.

Suddenly, before anyone realized, the country was in the middle of a devastating Depression. It was terrible to see everything slide downhill. In that dust-laden, moisture-less Badlands hell Pa struggled to keep his bank, his ranch, and his sanity. The Great Depression threw the country into a slump and people stopped buying, which caused a decline in prices, production, employment, and income. There was massive unemployment everywhere. Having never asked a penny from charity, self-reliant men now stood in long, gray-coated breadlines, afraid to go home empty-handed. Roosevelt came in and promised to change all that and the nation believed him. Will Rogers expressed the nation's confidence in the new President: "I will say one thing for this administration. It's the only time when the fellow with money is worrying more than the one without it."

In 1932, 273,000 families lost their homes through foreclosure. By January of the next year a thousand homes a day were taken over by mortgage holders. Small manufacturers and independent merchants were swallowed up and by 1933 over 85,000 businesses had failed. Rent signs were everywhere and every third store sat vacant. Nobody could collect fees and everyone was scrimping. Over six thousand banks, one quarter of the country's total closed their doors in 1932. Millions of Americans thought their life savings safely stored within the cool steel vaults of trusty neighborhood banks. The sudden betrayal and shock of losing all of their savings left people pounding on closed bank doors in rage. When the reality finally sunk in, they asked themselves if there was really anything left to believe in. The lucky ones were those old-fashioned souls who had stuffed their earnings in tin boxes and buried them in the backyard.

During informal radio broadcasts called "Fireside Chats" FDR assured the American public that his New Deal would save the country. On the evening of

March 12, 1933 his topic was banks:

I issued the proclamation for the nationwide bank holiday. The second step was the legislation passed by Congress to. . .lift the ban on that holiday gradually. . .There will be, of course, some banks unable to open without being reorganized. . .I do not promise you that every bank will be reopened or that individual losses will not be suffered. . .Confidence and courage are the essentials of my plan. You must have faith; you must not be stampeded by rumors. . .together we cannot fail.

One morning depositors found a note tacked to the front door of the bank in Scenic. Within an hour stunned farmers gathered in disbelieving groups to read the notice: "THE STATE BANK OF SCENIC IS HEREBY CLOSED." Whispers had it that the Nightrider had been seen leaving the back door carrying two large satchels the night before. Be that as it may, the bank failure wiped out the savings of depositors because the funds were not insured. Pa didn't believe in insurance. He went from banker to banker using every means within his scope to borrow money to prevent the $10,000 fine levied on the bank for insolvency. One of the more astute members of a local banking family in Rapid City who managed to survive the Depression without any investment of his own money and without noticeable difficulties, refused to grant Pa a loan. The loan would have averted, at least temporarily, the closing of Pa's bank, and more importantly the levying of the fine. With a tactless sneer, the banker told Pa, "Hell, Pete, you're too damned old to ever pay that off!" Years later during World War II, when cattle were high-priced, and manure on the boots was an unqualified passport to loans of any size, Pa had more money than he really knew what to do with, but help was impossible to get in the hayfields. This banker saw Pa on the street one day and jovially said, "Pete, I'll have to come down and help you put up that hay!" With sly malice Pa replied, "Hell, Driscoll, you're too damn old!" It took awhile, but revenge was sweet!

The bank examiners levied the huge fine on Pa and it nearly killed him. He ended up with a $60,000 debt, a crippling amount of money to owe during the Depression. In fact, debt was considered something of a disgrace, and upstanding characters didn't borrow money or buy on credit. Pa paid every last cent of the debt but he had to sell steers at eight cents a pound to do it. By the time he paid the last depositor, he was flat on his back in Rochester, Minnesota at Mayo Clinic. Brigadier General William James Mayo Jr. operated on Pa's bleeding ulcers. It was the only time in his life Pa ever let a doctor carve him up and it took a general to do it. When the government started buying cattle at ten dollars a head, and disposing of them in the quickest way possible, shootin' and buryin' them on the spot, it nearly did Pa in. Ma had been right, Pete Lemley was no banker, but he wasn't a debtor either.

The only good thing that came out of the Depression was Cake, a compressed piece of alfalfa, molasses, vitamins, protein, and everything else they threw in to keep a cow alive. It took a pound of Cake a day per cow and the great advantage of Cake was that it was easily transported. There was no need to use several teams and several hay racks and the labor to operate them. Just a few sacks of Cake in the back of the jitney, and after a few feedings, they could smell Cake a mile away!

Even though he'd lost his bank, Pa was still President of the School Board. There was a homesteader contingent on Holcomb Flat one year and they wanted to move the schoolhouse closer to their homes, about five miles closer. This would cost the taxpayers all of fifty dollars, but Pa felt it was a foolish expense. Homesteaders suffered from a natural attrition and would be gone in a short while. Pa knew he'd have to move that damn old schoolhouse back in no time. Besides, the school marm was mother. If the schoolhouse moved, Mama would have to travel eight miles a day; better the homesteaders' kids came half way and the schoolhouse stayed put. Pa knew that come election day the homesteaders would have the majority.

The basic means of transportation in that rough country were old spring wagons pulled by teams. The Nightrider rode again on a midnight gallop the night before the election and temporarily removed the horses from the Holcomb Flat area. By the time the puzzled homesteaders caught on, it was too late for the polls. The horses were returned quietly after another ride under cover of darkness and the school house slumbered on where it was. This lack of respect for opinions differing from his own didn't keep Pa awake nights.

As a dominant, and certainly the wealthiest member of a small western community, Pa always ran the election board. He took great pride in phoning his election returns before any other precinct got theirs in. With only a dozen or so votes to count, Pa was not adverse to setting his watch ahead a few minutes to accomplish this feat. During World War II Pa was dead set against Roosevelt and when he examined the ballots, which he felt a perfect right to do, most Roosevelt votes were dumped into the wastebasket because they had been improperly executed.

Many and deadly were the feuds engendered by school elections, and budgets were fought over with as much passion as politicians expend on billion-dollar appropriations. There were no salaried people involved in these arguments, just volunteers. As the largest taxpayer in the area, Pa was more concerned than most. Maggie always heard Pa bellyache about school board problems but one winter day Pa answered a phone call that got him roarin' mad. He got so hot Maggie just had to wait around to see what would happen next. "I'll tear your God damned heart out!" Maggie heard Pa growl into the phone.

"I've a notion to come down there and beat hell outta you," a man's deep voice boomed out of the phone.

"God damn it, Come on down you son-of-a-bitch!" Pa yelled, yanking the pipe out of his mouth. "You'll never leave here alive!"

This was too good to miss. Maggie stood behind the kitchen door as the big burly railroad section foreman pulled into the yard and slammed the car door shut with a bang! Out came Pa chargin' like a bull and the two grappled. They rolled over and over on the cold ground, a sixty-two year old wiry fox and a muscle-bound twenty-eight year old. First one got punched and then the other as Maggie watched with growing interest. They bit, spit, and kicked and the mouth-foamin' battle went on for ten cursing minutes until both men had pretty well beaten each other to pulps and lay sprawled on the ground gasping for breath. "Oh hell, we ain't gettin' nowhere," Pa said. "God almighty, let's go in and have coffee. There's no sense freezin' to death because we can't get along!" Maggie had to turn her back when the men came into the kitchen. It was sure mighty hard to keep a straight face when she asked each bruised and bleeding school board member which they wanted with their coffee, sweet roll or spice cake? Pa shot Maggie a glance and she knew it was time to clear out!

Pa took on women too. On one occasion a certain lady in the area (not a taxpayer) was expounding on the need to improve the schoolhouse. In her opinion, great renovations were in order such as painting the weatherbeaten boards, leveling the floor which had sunk in the corners, new desks, and more sanitary outdoor privies. Everyone in the room knew this lady didn't keep a clean house. Pa heard her out and then knuckling his mustache remarked, "Mrs. Smith, it just wouldn't do at all to make the outhouse so elegant; your kids might never want to go home!" The meeting adjourned in uproarious laughter, and the red-faced woman stalked out. The school outhouses remained dilapidated and nobody ever fell in.

The Badlands in our front yard

THE HIRED MAN

On July 27, 1931, a swiftly moving cloud covered the morning sun. South Dakotans looked up from their fields and were temporarily relieved. Summer temperatures scorched crops; ninety-five degrees was a cool spell compared to one hundred eleven and one hundred fourteen degrees for days at a time. Pennington County roads drifted over with blowing soil, dirt gritted between teeth, food tasted dusty, and noses clogged with it. During the dust barrage the region was stricken with epidemics of measles, strep throat, and other bronchial diseases that turned into dust pneumonia, a killing infection. Ponds, streams, springs, and wells went dry and the Missouri and Cheyenne Rivers sank lower than had ever been recorded, leaving cattle to walk paths a foot deep in dust. The endless days of hot wind might have been over had the moving cloud covering the sun been full of moisture for the parched earth and the thirsty living creatures below. Instead, the destroying cloud spread over five states and one hundred forty-six thousand square miles, an eerie whirring cloud of millions upon millions of grasshoppers.

Mama rubbed the sweat from her face with her apron as she bent over the stove, taking the last pie from the oven just before noon. The kitchen darkened suddenly, and she looked out the window at the apple orchard, her pride and joy. All summer she nourished the small orchard with every ounce of energy, carrying bucket after bucket of well water to the beloved trees pregnant with baby fruit, not the plump juicy apples of years past, but big enough to sell for new school shoes and the books Maggie loved so well. If only they could have just one good rain, even a short terrible South Dakota downpour, the kind that comes with pounding umbrella-breaking force driving every walking and creeping thing for cover.

By the time it dawned on Mother that the coming cloud was not a raincloud but a swarm of teaming, spitting, sticky grasshoppers, the monsters had already landed in the orchard. She grabbed a fly swatter and ran outside but before she got ten feet her hair was full of them. They crawled up her legs and inside her blouse, a mass of wiggling, jumping bodies. She ran back into the house, slammed the door shut, flung off her clothes, and stamped on them until nothing moved and the kitchen floor was littered with brown, crusty skeletons. Mama shuddered at the window while grasshoppers fed voraciously on her apple orchard, leaving it virtually bare. When the swarm finally lifted up into the churning air, even the bark on the apple trees had been eaten away.

The drought and the grasshoppers took their toll on Mama. She coughed endlessly, all day and all night, exhausted from the heat and the worry of how to put Maggie through high school now that Ray had graduated from Medical School and was out on his own. The children's welfare was the only thing that kept Mama going and she wasn't about to let Maggie miss out on a good education. So the two of them sat down and tried to figure out a way to make extra money.

Maggie sat next to her ice-cream stand on the main road leading to the ranch, a perfect place for thirsty customers travelin' to and from Rapid City, the Black Hills or The Badlands. Making ice-cream was no small job. Mama started out with clean ice. She made custard, pounded the ice fine and put it in a tub with a good deal of salt sprinkled in. After the ingredients were added and the lid put on the bucket, the real work began. The hired man twisted the pail with one hand, halfway round, then half-way back, tedious work turned the mixture harder until it froze. The sides were scraped and Maggie licked the spoon. They packed the vanilla ice-cream in a crock with cracked ice and hauled it out to the road under the cottonwood tree. Next to it Maggie set up a big sign that read: "MAGGIE'S ICE-CREAM – THE BEST IN THE WEST!"

Maggie leaned back to read Edna Ferber's best-selling western saga, Cimarron. She heard a car coming, sat up and waved, and the car slowed down to stop. The door opened and long legs in shiny, grey silk stockings got out. The woman walked over and leaned down to look at the ice-cream. Maggie was enveloped in a pungent smell of lavender perfume. "Hello! What a pretty little thing selling ice-cream on such a hot day. Now, that's just what I want." she said. Fanning her face with a lace handkerchief, the woman's filmy soft blouse clung to her full breasts as she breathed. She slipped the lace hanky down between her breasts and Maggie stared. She'd never seen a woman do that before. Maggie was lookin' down at her own flat chest when the woman asked, "How much is your ice-cream Maggie?" At the sound of her name, Maggie jumped.

The woman introduced herself as she licked the ice cream cone, twirling it slowly on her tongue. She was Violet Kasparie, a school teacher, looking for the President of the School Board to inquire about a job. "That's my Pa," Maggie said proudly, "But he won't be home till supper."

"Tell him I've come to see about a job, will you? Tell him I'll catch him another time." As she was walkin' off, she turned on high heels and said, "You make delicious ice-cream. Is that your mother's recipe?"

"Yep, Mama helped me."

Maggie watched as the car went out of sight. Within six hours, ten more customers bought ice-cream that was the best in the west. That night Maggie sat on the bed counting her money, the profit that was to mark the beginning of a long and successful business career and the end of her mother's life. For a couple of days Maggie practiced putting a handkerchief down her blouse but it fell right down through and bunched up just above her cowboy belt, so she gave it up.

The attractive Miss Kasparie was job hunting that summer of 1931 after losing her contract as school teacher at Spring Creek for the coming fall. When she first came she boarded with the Bradford family. It wasn't too often a married woman taught school and Mother was probably the exception because Pa was President of the School Board. Some areas of the country had strict rules that once a teacher married, she lost her job. After Miss Kasparie joined the Bradford household the oldest Bradford boy took a liking to the pretty school mistress and the feelings were apparently mutual. They began spending more and more time together and one Friday evening young Bradford announced that he was driving Miss Kasparie up to Deadwood the next day to see her relatives. He planned to stay with them and bring her back Sunday night. Mrs. Bradford, a proper lady, didn't think too much of her son going off for the weekend with a young woman, but since Deadwood was just a one-day trip, she guessed it was alright. The young couple left early Saturday morning, a bright, warm spring day. The Lilacs were blooming their sultry fragrance as they left the Bradford place heading north.

That same afternoon a team drove up to the Bradford place and a man came up to the door. Mrs. Bradford had her hands in flour and she wiped them on her apron as she pushed open the kitchen door. The man was dressed in clean work coveralls, a plain looking man with a small mustache. Mrs. Bradford noticed his rough hands and his limp, dragging one leg. He was polite, took off his old hat and spoke softly.

"Are you Mrs. Bradford, ma'am?"

"Yes, I am. Mr. Bradford and the boys are out in the barn if you've come to see him."

"No ma'am, I've come to see my wife."

"Your wife? I'm sorry, you must have the wrong place."

"Well, ma'am are you the Bradford's boarding the school teacher, Violet Kasparie Stout?"

"Why yes, . . . but there must be some mistake. Miss Kasparie is a single woman."

"No ma'am, that ain't right," the man explained. "I'm her husband. I'm a harness maker at Duhamels in Rapid and my Kasparie hasn't been home to visit me for over a month. I started getting worried . . . thought I should come down to see why."

Mrs. Bradford's face had turned a crimson red as she stared at the man in disbelief. "You mean . . . you can't mean Kasparie is married? She can't be. I . . ." Just then, Mr. Bradford came out of the barn and walked straight across the yard.

It was an embarrassing few minutes as Mr. Bradford explained that his oldest son had left for the weekend with Mr. Stout's wife! Ernie Stout had a cup of coffee with the Bradfords and then left, a saddened man. Living apart from his wife now for two years, he still hoped she would give up other men and come home to him and the five year-old child.

The Bradfords were shocked and outraged to think their son had been tricked into believing she was a single woman. Checking the Velvet Tobacco can under her son's bed where he kept five years of savings, Mrs. Bradford was not surprised to find it empty. She cried bitter tears, not only because of the scandal that was sure to follow, but for the boy who had fallen into a trap as old as man and womankind. She went directly to Kasparie's room and packed the woman's clothes. She found several bottles of L'Aimant Perfume, a fragrance that cost $1.00 per quarter ounce, an unheard of extravagance no ordinary school teacher could afford, and flimsy red unmentionables no decent woman wore. All of "Mrs." Kasparie Stout's belongings were sitting on the front porch when she and young Bradford pulled into the yard Sunday evening, all secret smiles and bashful looks. Their weekend romance was interrupted by Mr. Bradford's harsh demand that his son get the hell out of the car! Mr. and Mrs. Bradford never mentioned the unfortunate affair again, even to friends and neighbors. Their secret was safe for sixty years.

Violet Kasparie Stout was out of a job for the coming school year. She came lookin' for Pete Lemley when she heard the school teacher, Mrs. Grace Lemley was taking a year off on account of poor health. After thirty-three years of back-breaking work, Mama was advised by her doctor to spend the winter in Rapid City, to rest and avoid heavy lifting and long hours on her feet. Maggie was selling ice-cream to pay for her school clothes while Mama saved money from her fancywork to hire a housekeeper, a plain looking Polish woman named Bertie Klebe. Pa said he could get along at the ranch that winter with help from Mama's brother Roy Davis.

Mama lost her ninety-two year old mother that fall, the descendent of the grand old Peabody name. She reminiscenced about her mother, telling Maggie that she had been a hard-working and God-fearing woman without a grey hair on her head. The tiny ninety-five pound lady wouldn't have a car, preferring to hitch up old "Shorty" and drive into town to pay her taxes. When she couldn't find a hitchin' post anywhere, she complained to the Mayor and he told Grandma to tie her horses to the brass doorknob on the Court House instead.

Maggie loved Rapid City. Her pretty blond hair, slim figure, and devil-may-care exurberance attracted the boys in droves. Winter brought the latest Conga dances, ice skating, tobaggoning, sleigh rides, and parties instead of the usual ranch chores; choppin', haulin', carryin', and shovelin', all the work Maggie could do without just fine.

The cruel world of Depression that winter was replaced in Maggie's eyes with wonderful fantasy musicals, movies like "Flying Down To Rio," in which a row of sunny show girls danced on the wings of airplanes in flight. Mama saw to that. Kids got into movies for ten cents and theatres gave away door prizes. In 1934, double beds, long kisses, words like "hell" and "damn" were banned from films. Clean family pictures starring Shirley Temple, Mickey Rooney, and Marie Dressler were popular, although an undercurrent of gangster heros like Edward G. Robinson surfaced after the repeal of Prohibition in 1933. If it wasn't the Saturday matinees there was always radio, weekday evenings with the "Amos and Andy Show," and the funny pranks of Edgar Bergan and Charlie McCarthy.

The racking cough seemed better and Mama began to gain a little weight. During the weeks of much needed rest she began to write short stories. Mother's dream to write became a reality with this first restful opportunity. In January she sat in front of the comfortable fireplace and took out her $1.00 fountain pen. In large printed letters she underlined the title, "The Hired Hand, written by Josephine Lemley." She was moved to write that day after seeing a poignant magazine photograph of a tattered man with a bundle over his shoulder, a man she had seen many times before:

Published in a recent issue of the Chicago Herald, was a photogravure of an oil-painting "The Hired Hand." Truly it is a great picture. Even without the title, you know this man has worked faithfully, honestly and many years for some one else—words only cheapen the effect. But does the purchaser of this picture at One Thousand Dollars know its value in representing an extinct type, for nevermore will there be a person to sit for a like picture.

We are ranchers; not like some doctor who sets out to have a fancy pig-ranch, or a person who farms, or has a chicken-ranch, or even a dude ranch, but veteran ranchers who, for thirty years have put up hay summers and fed it out winters. And if we had pictures of all the "hired hands" during that time—some gallery!

Years ago hired men were of two classes, hoboes and tramps. And no one would have wished to borrow their clothes, but now the employees make the employer look shabby.

A good specimen of tramp was the old man who darkened the kitchen and only door, one June morning, asking for "a cup of tea mum". To keep on friendly terms with him, I prepared a nice lunch, at which he made a frightful grimace saying "Don't like tea. Rather have coffee."

Tramps never offered to pay and took but one meal in a place, so did not tire of the cooking. I later learned this was his third breakfast in the neighborhood.

The hobo might be any age, have any kind of habit, but he was a good worker—until he moved on. Hoboes and tramps are now replaced by the "Three in a Ford" variety, who come along and will

119

Threshing crew—date unknown.

work long enough to buy some gasoline. If they stay a week, one of them must start the Ford two or three times a day to be sure it will still run. Some morning they are off bright and early, not caring who puts up the hay. But another "Three in a Ford" will be along before night.

Mike, the Austrian, came but once. He never knew how much he could lift, and stacked hay all summer.

Then there was the Swede, who couldn't get up without being called. At one time he was the only man at home, the others being away on the round-up, so I decided to see if his boast were really true. I would not call him. He slept in the tent which was then our "bunk-house."

On my morning duties, at ten o'clock that hot July morning, and assured by the loud snoring, peeped in to see the flies in a grand procession in and out of his open mouth. Calling him was more sanitary.

The cowboy comes with his big chaps and spurs, a youth living up to his ideal. He cannot do much in the line of work, but if someone else will do the milking, he may stay awhile.

The man of the ranch away, in desperation I hear of a good man and telephone him to come. He must keep his two horses in the barn on an oat diet. This is not according to Hoyle or any other authority known to ranchers, so after the boss returned, this man appeared no more at the table.

The "Over Sunday" man comes Saturday night. In winter he sits by the stove except while eating or sleeping until Monday morning. He soon returns from his job at the wood-pile, and states that it is customary for the employer to outfit a man before he can work. He will need overshoes, cap, mittens and other clothes amounting to twenty-five dollars. He is invited to seek a new employer, which he does—muttering.

The next one comes with a suit-case and a great ambition to paint all the buildings at a very low cost. He has supper and bed, but leaves before breakfast to paint for some one down the road.

We hear of a man and wife who want to work. I go in a car fifty miles for them. It is raining, so they stack many bundles and suit-cases in the back and pile in. At the home gate, strange noises are heard. I look at them. They look at me. "O that's our little house-dog. Didn't you see us put her in? Forgot to speak about her." I had never before felt the need of a house-dog on the ranch. "Baby" had eyes somewhere under her long sandy-colored wool, and was about eight inches long, and of decidedly domestic habits. But besides taking excellent care of "Baby" and her six puppies this couple *worked faithfully for us.*

I have not mentioned the professional employee. He works a few days, and develops some malady. He must leave at once while the boss is away, and leave a small credit. He enters the hospital and has sent to us a bill of great length. Some of this variety may be enthusiastic enough to even break a leg. If you do not pay the bills they recover sooner.

Next, the particular one. He is middle-aged and begins by telling how his wife never could make jelly. She couldn't make cornbread to suit him. He always has some new information regarding things "not fit to eat."

About the same age is the "tree-specialist." If some smooth-speaking agent has induced the rancher to set out currant bushes or apple trees, the special "tree trimmer" can trim them so they will not bear for three years, and maybe never.

Once in thirty years a man may come along who is swift like the one I shall call Lightning. He was a fine honest fellow, and could do work five times as fast as any one else. Lightning would haul the water, be gone to some distant part of the ranch, before I discovered the barrels empty, the water having splashed out during the hasty trip from the spring.

Times changed. Ranchers built new houses, using the original "shack" for a bunk-house. Lightning was assigned the job of moving my fifty hens to the new place. In his haste he drove up a steep hill. The hens all slid back. In still more haste he hurried along before something might happen to those hens. In ten minutes he reached the new place, but thirty-six of the hens would never need more care — they were smothered. But altogether Lightning had many good points, and we were sorry to see him leave. When he left in a hurry to please his wife after the war all available employees were refugees from the law. Some would say they could work until a certain date when they must appear in court. The good ones would be picked from the job by the sheriff for forgery, car-theft or bigamy.

One Italian who had given bad checks until the banks wanted him, was captured by my husband, and he was sentenced to nine months in the State Penitentiary. As soon as that term was finished, back came Joe Columbus for a job. I was terrified, thinking he might be seeking revenge or a chance to burn us out. Husband of course, hired him and sent him into the house. Being without inside help, I was a busy woman. Joe looked things over and volunteered, "Churn butter, me." I put the cream into the barrel churn, probably more than I should have. Joe churned furiously without letting out the air, until off came that lid, treating Joe and myself to a rich shower-bath. Ceiling, stove, in fact the whole kitchen received some of the benefit. We looked at each other and laughed—and I was afraid no more. Joe's black eyes harbored no malice. But it took me nearly a day to clean and press his clothes.

Joe washed, cooked, set table, entertained the baby, squinted into the percolator and asked "Washum coffee-pot?" And he finished up at night by washing the kitchen floor. He stayed many days and helped as much as any girl could have done.

It is now customary to call the Farm Bureau Office when in need of help. The applicants guarantee nothing on their part, but if OUR references are satisfactory, they come and sample our food and decide.

We sometimes threaten to sell the cattle, and the whole outfit. But of what use would the money be with no hired help to pay! Yet we keep on, not knowing how to stop gracefully.

But it is only a matter of a few months until we shall hear a roar and a rush, some one at the door in cap, goggles and rain-coat asking for a job. We shall silently point to a vacant hanger near six occupied ones and prepare supper for one more on the hay-crew.

Several more stories followed that winter and Mama sent them out for publication, but each one came back rejected. Publishers were hardest hit during the Depression and were sticking with the work of known writers.

One bright March morning Mama and Maggie decided to visit the ranch. No one knew they were coming until they burst into the kitchen. Bertie the hired woman turned in fright and Mama was just as surprised. Plain Bertie was pregnant! On the trip home Mama blamed her brother Roy Davis for the unwanted pregnancy. Roy had been at the ranch all winter working for Pa. It must have been Roy. Who else could it have been?

When the baby boy was born Mama made sure the poor woman had plenty of baby clothes and toys for her little Billy. Mama tried to get Roy to marry the unfortunate woman, but Roy flatly refused. It was certainly unlike his usual gentlemanly behavior. Maggie's brother, Dr. Ray Lemley, brought home his new bride Myretta about that same time and perky Myretta commented to Maggie how much the hired girl's baby boy looked like Pa. Maggie looked him over but couldn't see a bit of resemblance. Years later when Roy died, a sizable inheritance appeared for the boy, which proved to Mama that she had been right all along.

DEADWOOD - 1930'S

DISGRACE

Grace Lemley brought her daughter back to the ranch in June of 1935, away from the alarming wave of crime that hard times had produced. Criminals were looking for easy money and the newspapers were filled with bloody stories of shootouts with the likes of murderer and bank robber John Dillinger. In Washington, D.C., J. Edgar Hoover headed the Federal Bureau of Investigation, a living folk hero of law enforcement. In quick succession his crimebusters nailed vicious Baby Face Nelson, Charles "Pretty Boy" Floyd, Arizona Clark "Ma" Barker, and kidnapper George "Machine Gun" Kelly. As if on cue, violence erupted across the United States with "Bonnie and Clyde" killings dominating front page headlines. Since aviator Charles Lindbergh's twenty month old son was kidnapped, the American press couldn't get enough of it and the Black Hills region of South Dakota was no exception. It was certainly time to go back to the peace and quiet of the ranch.

The winter rest in town restored Mama's spirit, if not her health, providing renewed energy for a good spring clean at the Circle Bar. She scrubbed, washed, aired out bedding, waxed and polished wood floors to a gleaming shine. The henhouse restocked and the cellar swept clean, freezers emptied, garden in, woodpile high, Mama stood back and admired her well-organized home. Nothing really gave her as much deep satisfaction as keeping her family well and happy, and her houses clean. Devotion to those priorities was the cornerstone of her life.

Although the ranch was back to normal, there was something different about Pa. For thirty-seven years Pa's vexing habits were difficult to live with but somewhat predictable. His wife and children knew he would be grouchy in the morning, that he'd complain about the cost of electricity, and demand the same hard labor he asked of himself. They didn't say workaholic in those days; they said hard worker. Around Pa everyone had to work hard in order to try and keep up with him. He drove himself to a point where most men would have collapsed from exhaustion. After operating on Pa for ulcers, Dr. Mayo had strongly advised a period of relaxation following meals and Pa usually stuck to that routine. As soon as Mama returned to the ranch, she immediately noticed that he wasn't doing that anymore. After the evening meal, and while Mother did the dishes listening to the radio show "Fibber Magee and Molly," Pa reached for his hat and was gone.

He was back for chores every morning, but Mama realized she was sleeping alone. She worked through all the motions of everyday life; cooking and smiling, washing and smiling, but vague demons floated around in her head. A constant sense of foreboding and uncertainty filled her days. At night she lay awake with the shadows of her married past searching for a reason her husband had left her bed. She was fifty-four years old, but looked much older, and her health was poor. Years of sun and wind, hot stoves and freezing wash water had carved the slavery of a young married wife into the face of an over-worked and prematurely wrinkled woman. Men call them character lines, but a woman knows better. No misunderstandings, no nagging, no harsh words; just acute and lonely isolation. Mama's Victorian dignity resisted the terrible temptation to ask Pa where he was going every night. The man she had worshipped, the only man she had ever loved and trusted more than any other, the man to whom she had given her energy and faithful devotion was now "cattin' around" with complete indifference. She wanted to scream, "When did you stop loving me?" but she couldn't bring herself to believe that perhaps Pa had never loved her. She wanted to stop him in the doorway, ask him point blank, but Mama knew he might rise up in anger against her. She'd already seen that side of Pa while Chauncey was still alive. Hearing a cry, the boy had run into the kitchen just as Pa raised his hand to strike her. The ten year-old jumped on Pa's back to defend his mother, grabbing his father's throat, "Don't you ever hit my mother! I'll kill you first!" With a quick twist, Pa threw the wiry child to the floor, but Chauncey leaped between them again, reaching across Mama with one arm, the other fist clinched defiantly in Pa's face. "You'll beat me now, but someday you'll pay for it!" he warned. But he was just a kid and couldn't back it up. He would have been thirty-four years old now, just when Mama needed him the most.

Ray and Myretta moved to Rapid City and Ray began a medical practice that would eventually gain him enormous respect in his field. He braved winter blizzards to deliver babies and was known to make house calls in an airplane if he couldn't get through on the roads. Myretta was a stylish woman whose face and body were connected to the most beautiful legs in town. Her bubbly personality and winning social graces made her a popular hostess and for years the Lemley's gracious home was a focal point for Rapid City's interesting social life. Myretta and her friends in the "Quaint Moderns Club" contributed more than their share to civic activities. Myretta Johnston Lemley came from a reasonably affluent North Dakota farm family, hard-working honest people, proud their daughter had married well. While Maggie was still too young to comprehend the sad, deep nausea of soul that was destroying Mama, Myretta sensed that something was terribly wrong with her mother-in-law. Mama wasn't eating properly, she didn't look well, and smiled much less often. Myretta invited Mother to parties, took her to movies, and saw that she joined the Eastern Star. None of her efforts did any good. "Grace, I think you should write," Myretta would say. "Write stories. You're sure to have one published one day." With that encouragement Mother began to write a little more but Myretta wasn't satisfied. She invited Mama to tea one morning and Myretta seized the opportunity to confront her. "What's the matter? Is there something you aren't telling me?" Myretta asked suddenly. After so much private torment, of holding in the secret she considered a disgrace and somehow her fault, Mama broke down.

"He's seeing another woman," she cried through blinding tears.

Myretta was instantly alarmed. "What do you mean? Who is?"

"Pete. He's sleeping with someone. He's never home at night."

Myretta sighed with relief that it wasn't Ray. She stopped drinking her tea in mid-air and looked across the table at a woman she was just seeing for the first time, a young woman in a very old body, a passionate being who had never hurt a living thing in her life. Although she remained outwardly calm, Myretta saw red; a bright, crimson, whorish, red. She came over and put her arms around her mother-in-law. "Don't worry Grace dear, it won't last. I can promise you that."

Without her husband's knowledge, Myretta began at once a furious investigation using discreet contacts to find out about "the other woman." It was a shock to think that a sixty-five year old grandfather sneaked around in the dead of night without caring if his wife knew or not. The myth of the faithful, settled older man had just about as much truth as the white knight in shining armor. It didn't take Myretta long to figure out what might happen to the ranch and to Pa's money if some woman played her cards right.

When Myretta finally discovered who Pa was "cattin'" around with she told her husband. To Ray, the ranch was the Holy Grail, his inheritance, his retirement, and his mother's blood and sweat (in that order). From that moment in the summer of 1935, when a German named Adolph Hitler was already gaining the awesome power that would ultimately effect the world, Ray Lemley began a war of his own. Myretta learned that a some-time school teacher separated from her husband, was bragging that she would soon have a new fur coat. The woman lived in the Sweeney Block on the third floor above Tom Sweeney's old Hardware Store.

For thirty-five years, single apartments in the red brick building were often rented by women of ill repute. Violet Kasparie lived down a dark seedy hallway in room 14. Men entering the long, dimly-lit hallways from the back, passed peeling wallpaper scribbled with faded messages, none of which were left by the disreputably respectable men, who didn't tarry out in the shabby linoleum hallway any longer than they had to. From the street, Kasparie's windows were always open. Shrill, empty laughter floated out over the second floor roof to the alley below, while a radio droned "Mississippi Moon" on warm summer evenings. When Mama found out where Kasparie lived, she stood in the shadows

Mama's house in town 1936.

and watched the sheer white curtains blow slowly out, then back, in the wind.

It wasn't a transient breeze that blew Grace Lemley into the private office of a Rapid City banker. She was there with a definite purpose; she wanted a loan. The banker looked at Mama in amazement saying, "Nobody is doing anything! This is a Depression!" Mother folded her white-gloved hands in her lap. "Well then," she said quietly, "I think its high time someone did something!" The result of Mama's visit to the bank president was the first FHA loan for a multiple dwelling house in Rapid City. The $14,000 loan wasn't bad considering a twelve room Italian Villa in elite Westchester County, New York cost $17,000 and a seven room Spanish bungalow in Beverly Hills, California cost $5,000. The three-family home was designed to rent with the finest hardwood floors, hot water heat, and window boxes that overflowed in the summertime with colorful fragrant flowers. Mama and Maggie would spend summers on the ranch and winters in town. The extra rental income meant shoes, school clothes, and books.

Deliberately shielded from her mother's private misery, Maggie enjoyed the social whirl of high school parties and sports activities, of handsome beaus, of enjoyable teenage fun. Mother had planned it that way. She loved seeing her daughter happy, enjoying a carefree young life. Nothing ever showed on Mama's face and not a word was mentioned about the greatest disappointment in her life. Newsy letters to Libby told only that she moved to town in the winters for her health: "I keep in practice by moving twice a year. When you live two places, you never have anything either place. I am taking boarders, four teachers are two in a room and pay $30 a month each. We have the same woman at the ranch we have had three years. (Bertie and mysterious child) Maggie needs a new pair of shoes but will have to wait."

By fall, the scandal crawled out of the closet. Maggie was ready for the University of Wyoming and Myretta thought it was time to tell her the truth before she left. Ray Lemley was humiliated over his father's bold dalliance with a woman like Kasparie, especially during a time when Ray's medical reputation was becoming increasingly important. Ray was establishing a major clinical practice, the first Rapid City physician in private practice to do so. His clinical experience would someday help develop the Rapid City Medical Center, a lasting tribute to years of devoted patient care. Ray's early experiments with the element Selenium in animals and humans was the basic step for some forms of cancer research. Besides his mother, Dr. Lemley had the most to lose. Instead of creating a public scandal, which might have destroyed Ray's plans and created a humiliating social embarrassment for the whole family, Ray, Myretta, and now Maggie, with Mama the reluctant participant, decided to catch Pete Lemley and Violet Kasparie Stout red-handed. If Pa could be caught with his pants down, it might teach him a lesson and scare the brazen woman away.

Pa was led to believe that everyone in the family would be spending the weekend in town for a party at Myretta's. Mama and Maggie packed up and left after lunch, waving goodbye to Pa as they drove past him sitting on his horse in the corral. They went to Rapid City and picked up Ray and Myretta, and together the fearless foursome returned to the ranch in the dead of night. They left the car a half mile away and walked quietly to the house. The moon was covered by clouds, the night warm and sultry, perfect weather for a raid on the Badlands Fox. Ray checked and found Kasparie's old car hidden in the barn so they knew the time was right for the kill. As silently as possible, the kitchen door opened and four nervous people and one dog entered the house. At that moment Maggie saw her parent's bedroom door closed on the main floor but she could plainly hear hurried steps on the stairs leading to the second floor bedrooms. She and her dog "Pat" bounded upstairs, jerked open a bedroom door, and pulled on the light chain. There lay Kasparie pretending to be asleep under the covers. Several seconds later loud thumps resounded on the stairs, thump! thump! Kasparie's head hit the second floor landing below the diamond shaped window. There was a great snarling struggle, and in between barks, "Pat" bit Kasparie's feet. Maggie dragged the screaming woman down the stairs. Kasparie squirmed and spit like a snake but Maggie had fistfuls of hair twisted around her wrists. Kasparie's silken negligee tore open and her nearly naked body landed with an awful thud on the floor at Mother's feet. Mama stood there like a statue as the cursing woman got up and ran out the back door to her car and drove off, the faithful dog "Pat" close on her heels. By then, everyone else was out in the yard and crafty Pa knew the worst was over. He came chargin' out of the house with gun in hand. He shot at Myretta's feet, only Myretta's, ignoring his wife and children standing near-by. It was Myretta's legs he wanted, her beautiful legs. But he didn't kill any-body, just swore and told them all to go to hell, shot a few more times to see Myretta jump, and went back to bed.

Ray took his scared wife and trembling mother back to town but Maggie yelled at Pa that she was staying at the ranch! After it was all over, she found herself out of breath alone in the yard, still clutching matted handfuls of long brown hair.

The next morning Maggie woke up congratulating herself. She'd run Kasparie off for good! She walked out on the back step to feed her dog, yawned, and turned around to go in. It was then she noticed Pa's bedroom window screen was off and leaning against the house. As soon as Maggie had gone to bed, ex-hausted from the ugly kitchen scene, someone had left her car down the road and crept silently back into the house.

THE LAST ANNIVERSARY

Ray exhausted himself trying to run a medical clinic at the same time he was launchin' surprise raids on Pa. No tellin' how many times Pa out-maneuvered him and Ray was gettin' nowhere. The more times Ray was foiled, the madder he got. At the rate he was goin', there wouldn't be a Circle Bar Ranch left by the time Ray retired and was ready to do what he really loved doing, being a rancher like Pa. He always needed to be as good as Pa in every respect to prove to Pete Lemley that his only remaining son was as good a rancher as he was. Ray was a wonderful doctor but that particular need, to best Pa at ranchin', was never to be.

For experimental purposes, Ray kept a pen of rattlesnakes at the ranch in case of the need for venom. Everyday the snakes had to be fed milk with a syringe. Pa thought that was a breeze. One morning at dawn he went out and lifted up the lid on the snake pen. It wasn't light enough and while he was feeding one snake another rattler, disturbed from sleep in its resting place, lunged and bit Pa on the thumb. Now Pa had been bit by just about everything and had doctored many a horse with snake bite. He knew the first and most important thing was the mental element. Panic and shock after a rattler bite can make a person faint dead away. A man out by himself who gets weak in the stomach and faints after a snake bite loses the precious time he needs to save himself. The fang puncture bled immediately, but not ten seconds after Pa was bit he cut two long incisions directly through the fang punctures. He sucked out the blood and venom, spit and sucked some more. He sucked the killing venom and spit for nearly an hour, sometimes seeing everything yellow around him, an eerie sensation. There had been an almost immediate burning pain in his hand and by the time a hired man found him, the arm was swollen and badly discolored. Pa refused to go to the hospital, refused even to call Ray. He'd been shot twice and lived and if a snakebite wasn't bad enough, he wasn't about to get stabbed with a needle!

Pa was laid up nearly a week. The pain was terrible, and his arm swelled up with huge, black shiny blisters of infected, oozing blood, some so large he couldn't recognize his fingers from his hand. His scalp tingled, his mouth went

Dr. Ray Lemley after retirement

numb and he sweat buckets. The fang punctures oozed blood for days and Pa's gums bled. By the time Ray found out several days later, Pa was out of danger and sittin' up with his pipe. Hell, no! He wasn't goin' to no damn hospital! He drank water in great gulps; couldn't get enough water. Ray figured Pa wouldn't have made it if he hadn't been in such good physical shape. He made it through the ordeal but the rattlesnake probably died from the bite. It may well have been that Pa got well quicker because he had help from a cheap private nurse.

Maggie was tired of ranches, snakes, and women vipers. She wanted to attend the University of Wyoming in the fall of 1936. She didn't like leaving when Pa was neglecting his family but her mother could see into the future, encouraging Maggie to make a life for herself: "I want you to learn to take care of yourself, to earn your own money. I don't ever want you to end up in a situation like I'm in." Maggie asked what Ma was goin' to do about Pa. "Oh, don't you worry, someday, some woman is going to make a fool out of him!" she said. Mama was monogamous to her deepest core but she didn't drown in despair or self-pity. She knew there was a fine line between enslavement and devotion. If her days were full of black emptiness, she kept them to herself. The deceit had been the hardest part, the death of trust. All the things she and Pa had lived through together, the struggles they had endured, all the back-breaking work that now seemed so meaningless. Perhaps she had made her husband too much the center of her Victorian world, but the world had changed and women couldn't do that anymore. The only thing she wanted was to make sure her children weren't cheated out of the ranch she had worked so hard to buy and maintain.

Mother wrote faithfully to Maggie and sent her every penny she could scrape up, neglecting herself in the process.

> *My Dear Little Shrimp,*
>   *I just about have the flu today, but won't admit it, even to myself. That Kasparie hangs around Mrs. Vic's photography studio. She told Mrs. Vic she wants her to photograph a nude of her, says she has a good body. I don't see why not, as Mrs. V. likes to make money!*
>   *Your hopes, that I am on a big financial deal to make us rich, are not likely to materialize. I tried keeping count of my expenditures, until I was overcome with so many kinds of taxes and expenses.*
>   *Remember I'm always thinking of you and you are my one big interest in life. I'm so lonesome, I'm numb. Don't even care what Pa says or anything else. It is a good feeling tho, not to care.*

But Mama had cared too much. After Maggie left, Ray noticed that his mother was losing weight. He decided to get rid of Kasparie one way or the other,

Myretta Lemley in later years.

bought out, carried out, or run out, but she was going. He and Myretta devised yet another elaborate plan to catch Pa in bed with Kasparie, with witnesses, so that Mama would have grounds for divorce. Only one thing would keep Pa away from Kasparie, the thought that he might lose the ranch in a divorce. Ray knew Pa would rather have his fingernails pulled out one by one than lose one acre of his first magnificent obsession, the Lemley Circle Bar Ranch.

Acting on a tip from Kasparie's wretched husband, still pathetically waiting in the wings, Ray, Myretta, and Mama walked down the third floor hallway past the peeling wallpaper in the Sweeney apartment building. Mother stood back for a few seconds listening to a radio playing soft music somewhere in the building. It was all so sordid, to acknowledge the shame Mama had tried bitterly to forget. Everything seemed to happen then in slow motion. Ray kicked in the door, boards splintering, while people stuck their heads out of rooms up and down the hall. Pete Lemley quickly made his escape by jumping out of the bedroom window onto the second story roof below. Mama was standing next to the hall window and glanced down at her husband's graceful, foxlike leap from the roof to the alley. But this time Ray had anticipated Pa's escape route. A policeman quickly stepped out of the shadows to greet Pa, "Well hello Pete!" he whistled, "How's the weather up there?" There was no better witness than a policeman in a divorce court.

Ray's lawyers drew up the divorce papers asking for the entire ranch on grounds of proven adultery. Judge Harold Hanley and both lawyers were Ray's close friends so Pa never had a chance at anything resembling justice and he didn't deserve any. Ray had the whole thing worked out beforehand and it went exactly as planned, quietly settled out of court in Judge's chambers. Pa was either going to lose his entire ranch in an ugly divorce on grounds of adultery, or he would have to agree to deed half the ranch to Mama, which included a legal Will leaving her half to Ray and Maggie. He would also have to promise never to see Violet Kasparie again. In return, Mama agreed not to divorce him and break up the ranch and Pa could run the ranch as he saw fit. Judge Hanley wanted Mother to take half the cows but she refused saying, "a man has to have control of his livestock to sell when the time is ripe to sell."

Pa went back to the ranch in a huff and Mama returned to her quiet home in town for the winter. She wrote to Libby, who must have sensed a sad change in Mama. Although she never wrote a word about the ugly scenes she was trying to forget, Mama's letters were full of clues: "Pete is in Rapid City betting on the races the last three days. Wish someone would kidnap me and treat me well."

When Maggie came home on Christmas break from college, Mama had written a novel. She shyly held it out to Maggie and asked her to read it. The young woman had a million things she would rather have done but she sat down

1936—The year Mama died.

at the kitchen table and reluctantly read eight or nine pages. She thought it was awfully boring. The plot was too simple. A rancher lived with his wife and children on the banks of the Cheyenne River. The mother was made to work and no one noticed or appreciated the love and tenderness she had given them. The children went off and the greedy rancher only cared about his land and his money. The wife was suddenly kidnapped by Indians and the husband tried a long time to get her back. They finally found her safe at last and brought her home; the woman hoping that surely now they would realize how much they needed her. But everything returned to the same ordinary routine, the husband with his land, the children with their friends and the wife. . .well, Maggie didn't have time to find out what happened to the wife because she had to get ready to go to a Christmas party. She left the manuscript on the kitchen table open to page ten and hurried off to dress.

Not long afterward, Mother went back to the ranch one weekend to get a few things. The house was empty when she arrived, or so she thought. She was in the parlor when she heard a commotion and looked into the kitchen. She walked past the stove and over to the window that faced the old log cabin where she'd spent so many hard and lonesome years. Pa was standing next to a big pile of something and he lit it on fire. Flames shot up in the air and Mama watched little pieces of paper float upward in the yellow, licking flames. Suddenly, she came nearer the window to look closer at the pile. Across the yard she could see a hired hand leaning against the shed, dejected. Pa was cursing, "There'll never be another book on my place! None of you is ever goin' to stay up all night wastin' my electricity reading a damn book!" The flames shot higher and Mama stood by the window, tears streaming down her cheeks. All of Maggie's books, all of her own books, some handed down in the Peabody family, Thomas Henry, Jack London, James Oliver Curwood, Horatio Alger, all the sets of Maggie's Books of Knowledge Mama had saved so long and hard for. The flames licked the pages of the novel Mama wrote about the rancher and his family on the Cheyenne, early editions of Dickens, and Harriet Beecher Stowe; blowing them like all the tiny fingers that had turned them, burning with them the years of loving, butter churning, fancywork sewing, washing, teaching, driving, and leaving; purified and sacrificed into the cloudless sky.

Less than two months later, on March 1st, 1936, Ray phoned Maggie that he was sending a car for her to come home from college immediately. Mama was critically ill. Maggie arrived in Rapid and went straight to her mother's hospital room. When she looked in, Grace saw the movement from her oxygen tent. "Oh Maggie, what are you doin' home?" she asked.

"Spring break, Ma," Maggie lied.

"Now you just wash your hair and do anything you want to do," Grace told her. "I don't want you to get bored."

Mama worried that Maggie wouldn't be comfortable; always worrying about everyone else but never herself. Surprisingly, Pa was there too, no doubt prodded by Ray, and whenever he got up to move around, Mama's eyes followed him everywhere. On March 2nd before midnight, fifty-seven year old Grace Lemley, pioneer wife and mother, died gasping for breath on her thirty-eighth wedding anniversary. Not one person in the family remembered that it was her special day.

On a dismal day an occasional snowflake drifted down into the hole that would hold my mother's tired body. I looked across her open grave straight into Mr. Bergman's face and the tears were streaming from his eyes. Then I looked at my father and saw that he wasn't crying.

In shock, I went to Mama's silent home, walked absently through the dark kitchen, into the hallway and up the stairs to her bedroom. Standing near the closet holding my mother's robe to my face, I tried to smell her wonderful sweet smell. It would have taken so little time to read her novel, only a few minutes. I know it must have meant so much to her. I glanced over at the vanity, the ivory combs and brushes, the treasured box covered with tiny prairie stones a naughty little girl had made in the fourth grade, the delicate hand-painted figurine of a boy and his dog. Stuck in the mirror next to her Bible, I found a note written in my mother's familiar hand:

My Dear Little Shrimp,
How long will it take you to know that nothing really matters?
Things come and go, but there's an end to all things, and more
coming along. You must learn to live with good and evil, innocence
as well as sin, because nothing exists without its reverse. Don't
forget that a delightful experience is just around the corner. Grab
all the fun you can!
Your loving Mother

A FEISTY BRIDE

It's a wonder I didn't kill Pa. For five months I stayed out of his way, walked out of the rooms he walked into, ate by myself and ignored his existence. Ray must have felt the same way because he and Myretta left for the University of Vienna and were still there in 1938 when Adolph Hitler's troops seized the country and announced the union of Austria and Germany. In March and April 1938 Ray took photographs of the German occupation and smuggled them out. They proved to be the only existing photos at that time of Nazi occupation. He and Myretta then moved to Budapest while Ray studied Urology at the University of Hungary. During his studies Ray was instrumental in the removal of many refugees before the German Blitzkrieg. When Hitler's desire for world rule and the coming threat to allied nations caused international concern, Ray and Myretta got out while the gettin' was good and returned to the states. I was glad to have Myretta back. She held the family together—holiday dinners with all the trimmings, and her unfailing interest in my clothes, social life, and boyfriends. Up to that time Myretta was the only one in the family who could get money out of Pa. She even made Pa hop to it on occasion with her strong personality and principles. I would have had a dull life after Mama died, if it hadn't been for Myretta's great kindness.

Meanwhile, Pa waited until one stifling August afternoon, a day with no breeze, the car door so hot I couldn't touch it and he says, "Sissy, why don't we take a nice vacation to where there's some snow?" I gave him the dirtiest look I could muster, and he says, "God, yes, Sissy, why don't we just get in the car and head for Yellowstone National Park?" I watched the flies buzzing around the back screen door, waves of heat rising above the ground. I could just hear Mama say "Go on Margaret, grab all the fun you can. I worked myself to death so you could have this ranch." I turned to look into his sharp blue eyes and I said, "That sounds like a good idea Pa. There's a big geyser there I want you to see. Its called 'Old Faithful.'"

At Yellowstone I watched him feed the bears and I imagined one biting his head off. He had a great time with other women tourists we met but he was bored stiff with the gently flowing hot springs, the cool waterfalls, and the famous Old

Pa at Yellowstone National Park.

Faithful Geyser that gushed a huge stream of boiling water more than one hundred feet into the air. We walked around the hot, bubbling springs and I hoped he'd fall in, but he didn't. On the drive home I wanted to ask him if he still saw Kasparie, but I held my tongue. I'd heard she took off for Wyoming after she found out Pa wasn't goin' to give her a fur coat. Although I made deliberate references to Mama all the time, Pa never said a word about her, except to make the off-hand remark, "She made good donuts."

For the next couple of years I ended up workin' like a mule for Pa. Three times in the spring we'd round up cattle and make the twenty-four mile drive to summer pasture. Early mornings, 3 a. m. would find us in the yard tying up our tarpaulins to put on the pack horses. It was always misting slightly, and cold. It often turned into rain, but usually cleared when the sun came up. Ahead of us were many weary miles trailin' cattle. When it was cows and calves, it was a triple distance, travelin' back and forth behind them. The little ones got so tired they had to be frightened with a rope to keep their heads pointed in the direction their mothers were going. When they broke back, they all followed the leader, heading to their bed ground where they last saw "mama." Then it was pandemonium! A good husky calf could outrun our horses for quite a distance and we went after them as fast as we could. The herd had to be circled constantly until they were turned around. We camped overnite, and the boys took turns watching the cattle. I was the cook so I continued working after dark and at night I had to sleep on the hard wood floor of a claim shack listening to the loud snoring of all those smelly men. In the Badlands summer pasture we had to "mother" up the calves and stay with them until all had found their mothers and gone off with them. In the Fall we repeated the same maneuver back home for winter. It was usually around the first of November when we started home, and it always seemed cold and raining, or snowing. We were lucky not to get caught in an early blizzard. If a storm hit, it was hell ridin' around snow banks, and over bushes. Ice formed on Pa's mustache, he'd turn in the saddle and glare at me, "Mighta knowed something like this would happen when that damned Roosevelt got elected!"

Summers were just as bad, raking hay in over one hundred degree temperatures, long, grueling hours Pa never seemed to mind. He leased thousands of acres and the Badlands walls made fencing unnecessary. The Badlands looked dry, bleak and sun-baked, but the cattle always came out fat and sassy! The only time I ever heard him complain was one summer when the temperature was one hundred and twelve degrees. There were no trees or protection of any kind from the glaring, merciless sun. Sweat rollin' down his face, Pa says, "God Almighty, if this keeps up I'll have to take off my long underwear!" Pa wore longjohns all year 'round.

In 1938 my brother Ray invited a young physician, George R. Bodon, to join his clinic staff. George was from Budapest, Hungary but he was made a

141

I watched him feed the bears and I imagined one biting his head off.

Pa with Don Patton in front of the woodpile.

Left to right: Ray Lemley, Charles O'Rourke, August Ballman, Earl Taylor (the Wolf),

Pete Lemley (the Badlands Fox), Guy Taylor (Watcheye).   *Courtesy William R. Lemley, Sr.*

"Tiny" Singleton with "Satan" – 1940.

U.S. citizen in 1943. To make a long story short, I met the handsome doctor over the Christmas holidays and we fell in love. It was difficult to stay on the ranch when I'd have preferred being in town. It was along about that same time that I got into the biggest fight I ever had with Pa. It wasn't about Dr. Bodon, either. I was studying at night and the electricity bill showed a thirteen cent increase over the previous month. Pa hit the ceiling! I could go out with anyone I wanted to, but nobody was allowed to keep a light on after nine o'clock on the ranch – I had committed an unpardonable sin. After Pa switched the electricity off at night, I'd sneak down and turn it back on. I got caught when he saw the thirteen cent bill. He went crazy and bellyached for three days over that huge bill. Pa never said be honest, be true, be loyal, or be trustworthy. He just always told me, "If you get caught doin' something wrong, don't say you followed someone else. Tell them you did it yourself. You were the leader." So I told him I was studying after dark and he blew up, "This is my house and I always keep my bill under the minimum!" As it turned out, I was the only one who ever stood up to Pete Lemley and spit right in his eye!

I had to find a hired woman to keep up the ranch so I could lead my own life without having to ask Pa for money. He already had a good hired man. In all the years Virgil Post worked for Pa, they never got along one day in all that time. Virgil cussed Pa up one side and down the other and Pa took it. One day the cook, Ella Moore, packed a lunch and was going to take it down to the timber for Pa. Virgil was just goin' out the door and says to her, "Next time you go lookin' for that old man, you take an axe, don't take no cold milk!" Ella was a wonderful cook and she would've stayed longer but the boys found out she had killed someone and spent time in prison. Sometimes they'd tease her about it. One of Pa's hands and a good friend for forty years, Chuck Strehlow, made a sly remark to her one afternoon. Wham! She threw a fryin' pan at him. "You son-of-bitch!" she yelled. She was a tough western woman and when she left, I had to cook.

Hired help was hard to find but one afternoon I saw a young woman sittin' in the bus depot in Rapid City looking helpless and forelorn. She was the perfect type; completely naive, a homeless woman with just the shirt on her back, having lately gotten out of a bad living situation. I asked her if she wanted a job. Boy, did she! I took "Tiny" Singleton back to the ranch that she called home for the next seven years. She worked hard, even went out into the fields to work next to the men and I was glad to have her. So was Pa.

I had more on my mind than Pa's hired help. My fiance Dr. Bodon wouldn't take no for an answer. Pa came up to Ray and Myretta's lovely home in Rapid City to give his only daughter away in marriage. Pa was probably just as glad to get rid of me so that his electricity bill wouldn't exceed the minimum.

The night before the wedding I went up to mother's attic and lifted the lid of an old wooden trunk. The lid stuck tight and I pried it open. At once my mother's scent of orange and rosewater danced in the air around me and I reached into silken ribbons, between filigrees of delicate Victorian lace and brought out Grandmother Peabody's black-haired china doll. I put it aside with a copy of "Godey's Lady's Book," reaching deeper down, almost to the bottom of the trunk before I found it. I held my mother's lavender wedding dress up to the attic light, took off my clothes and put it on. For a few moments Mama and I danced into married life with as many high hopes and wonderful expectations as had all the brides before us.

THE BOMBS OF WAR

Shortly after my marriage FDR told Americans, "I have said this before, but I shall say it again and again: Your boys are not going to be sent into any foreign wars." We were all so preoccupied with our own lives that a second world war seemed as remote as the man in the moon. I was much more interested in Margaret Mitchell's *Gone With The Wind,* a romantic novel of the old South released as a movie in 1940. Now that was something to grab my attention!

Nazi dictator Adolf Hitler forced Americans to face the fact that he now controlled all of western Europe with only Britain and a wide ocean between Germany and the United States. In August, CBS war correspondent Edward R. Murrow broadcast live from London. My husband and I listened to the radio; the wail of air raid sirens and the scream of German bombs over London. On December 7, 1941 all hopes for peace were blasted when the Japanese attacked Pearl Harbor! My surgeon-husband immediately joined the 34th Evacuation Hospital overseas to chase around with General George Patton.

We were living in New York then and I was homesick for the prairies of South Dakota. The constant noise and rain, the dirty snow, and oily smoke from buses and trains, the pushing crowds all convinced me that the Circle Bar was the place to live after all. An urgent phone call from Myretta hurried the process along:

"Maggie, you have to come home! Tiny is trying to get the ranch!"

"Tiny? How?"

"She wants Pete to marry her."

"What's new about that? She's been mad over him for seven years."

"This time she's given him an ultimatum. Ray says you'd better come home."

It was the same story with a new twist. Pa was as spry as a cricket at age seventy-four. How women suffered when they fell in love with the Badlands Fox! Poor little Tiny, that trustworthy fighter thought Pa was a great man. As inconsistent as he was, Pa always had a woman around him who worshipped the ground he walked on. He never gave them a nickel, never took them anywhere, and agitated them to death. One minute they loved him and the next they wanted to kill

149

him. His magnetic, cagy, fearless personality left a trail of women and Tiny was just the next in line. Pa considered kindness and sudden generosity weaknesses and he was never guilty of either. The closer women got to him, the worse he became.

Alleluia! I was back to the Buffalo Grass, the constant sunshine, the cows, and the crisis! Seems Pa had promised Tiny back in 1937 that if she worked for seven years at four dollars a week, he would give her the deed to a one hundred and sixty acre ranch on Kube Table. She should have gotten it in writing. Of course, by then she'd fallen in love with the wily rascal and a roll in the hay became a routine part of the unwritten bargain. She had worked as hard as any man on the ranch those long seven years, cooked, cleaned, washed, put up hay; an indentured servant without a legal contract. Tiny had even paid for Pa's groceries out of milk money from her little herd of dairy cows! When Tiny's seven years were up she asked him for the earned deed to her ranch. "Ranch, what ranch?" Pa said. That good-natured patient woman would have made Pa a faithful wife if Myretta, Ray, and I hadn't stepped in. When Tiny saw that Pa had no intention of carrying out his half of the bargain, she gave him an ultimatum: "Marry me or I'm leavin'. " At that point, Ray poked his nose in and they got into an argument. Tiny started to pack up and Pa tried to talk her into stayin'. She told Pa she loved him so much that she'd sign a pre-nuptial agreement; she didn't give a damn about his money! But Ray and Myretta would have none of it. "Get the hell out of this house!" I heard Ray shouting at Tiny. "You were nothing when we found you and you're still a gutter rat!"

I sat on the porch in Mama's wicker rocking chair, the one she bought when Pa refused to let her have a bank account, listening to the argument in the house. I looked out over the sweet-smelling lilac bushes along the walk, remembering the way she smoothed my hair, her soft voice as she read to me from O. Henry's *To Him Who Waits:*

> *I sold my happiness for money. . .but that does not excuse me. . .I could not see then that all the money in the world cannot weigh in the scales against a faithful heart.*

Rocking there in my mother's arms, in her memory, I knew that Pa didn't deserve Tiny's love any more than he had deserved Mama's devotion. The voices got louder in the house, first a little begging voice, then a rough shout and finally Ray hit Tiny and she fell hard to the floor. I didn't hear Pa say a word. Ray threatened to break up the ranch, the same method he used to get rid of Kasperie. It was a bluff that worked on Pa because the ranch came before anything else in the world. If Pa had really loved Tiny, he'd have stepped in to defend her, but he didn't. We knew then we had him over a barrel.

Tiny moved to the ranch on Kube Table anyway, even though she knew she'd never get the deed. She taught school for a little while but the men swarmed

In the

around a woman living alone on the prairie. Pretty soon she got herself a husband and moved to Arizona. Tiny Singleton probably never realized what a favor we did for her.

Pa made life hell for all of us then. Ray was in Rapid City after discharge from the Army Air Corps and he didn't have to take the daily punishment. Pa clutched his purse strings even tighter than before and I spent a goodly parcel of my own money on groceries rather than ask him for anything! Of course, I was no more clever than the ladies before me...I worked like a slave, cooking, keeping house, galloping when needed, washing and ironing, and raking in the hayfield. After a full grueling day of outside labor, it was always expected I'd cook the meals too.

At that point I was saved by a desperate small town high school. Teachers were impossible to find, particularly out in the country, and especially at this school where the kids gave teachers a bad time. Now this was right up my alley! I'd been the same kind of kid while I was in school, just as ornery as the best of them. They'd met their match. There were four boys and three girls and I started out the year by giving the boys "loaded" cigarettes. As soon as they exploded in their little faces, I knew I had control.

I drove thirty-eight miles a day to school and the greatest blessing was that I didn't have to cook at the ranch. Somehow I convinced Pa that he must hire a cook, and not for four dollars a week either.

While he was losing Tiny, Pa was reaping the benefits of war! During World War II, Pa kept his cattle on the gunnery range that had once been part of the Pine Ridge Reservation. The "bomber ranch," as some of our older Indian neighbors called it, was the big Aerial Bombing and Gunnery Range established in 1942 along the north side of the reservation. The War Department ordered all whites and Indians to vacate the range by July 31, 1942, just three weeks to clear out. All the land lying on the south side of the Big White River to the south of the Badland's towns of Scenic and Imlay would be used for bombing from the air. The land south of Interior and Coneta would be used for gunnery practice. They'd be shootin' with .50 caliber machine guns from planes at large low targets made of screen and painted white.

Indians whose homes were in that fateful area lost nearly everything they had because they had no time to round up cattle and horses and nowhere to store household goods even if they had money to store it. Most of them ended up leaving everything and relocating with relatives on other parts of the reservation. White people scurried around trying to move furniture, headin' out in wagons loaded down like pioneers with boxes, trunks, children, and household animals. A government appraiser came out to set the fixed price for the land but the correct payments were always a matter of questionable amounts. It was a time of heartache and despair for many who had lived in the area all their lives.

Pa was overjoyed to see them all go! To him the gunnery range meant fifty miles of "free" pasture with the added benefit of "abandoned" cattle and horses added to his herd. Just as in W.W.I, Pa wasn't afraid of government restrictions one little bit. All that "free" pasture land looked real good to a rancher with a hungry bunch of cattle. In fact, the twenty-five percent penalty Pa had to pay if he got caught on the gunnery range was a drop in the bucket compared to what it would cost to lease the same amount of land. All we had to do was stay out of the way of bombs!

The only close scrape we ever had with a bomb was one afternoon when "Big Chuck" and I were out movin' cattle. The cattle were headin' slowly across the range about fifty feet from us when I heard the drone of a plane comin' in. With no time to duck for cover, and none there anyway, a bomb skittered across the ground and exploded in the cattle. Bam! Smoke, rocks, and dirt went up twenty feet, and everything that went up came crashing down around us! Our horses reared up, and cattle scattered in all directions. Luckily, neither one of us lost our horse and we only had a couple of cows with some strange, new government brands.

Later we heard a story about another fella on the bombing range who wasn't quite so lucky. He was out on his horse goin' home for the day and he passed by a small bridge. Under the shadow of the bridge drinking his fill from a stream, was a big old Hereford bull. The bull raised his head and saw the cowboy, snorted, and pawed the dirt. The fella didn't pay much attention until Blam! a bomb hit the bridge and splattered it flat. The next thing this fella sees when he comes to, is that his horse has run off and he's lookin' straight up into the fiery-red eyes of the maddest bull in the Badlands!

Pa in the Badlands

LET 'ER RIP!

World War II was over. Fathers, husbands, and lovers were whistling "You'd be so nice to come home to." We welcomed our men with the GI Bill of Rights and new gadgets like television. Before we knew it, Hopalong Cassidy, Arthur Godfrey, and Frank Sinatra were everyday names in our lives. All the things we'd missed; nylons, cigarettes, sugar, gasoline, tires, canned goods, and coffee were now available again. Bah! Pa got along just fine one way or the other and he'd taken full advantage of the war, adding hundreds of cows and thousands of acres to his already enormous Circle Bar.

I was glad to have my surgeon-husband home from the war in one piece, but I dreaded returning to rainy, depressing New York. My husband needed a back operation and a helpmate to rebuild his medical practice so there was no question about going. I gave it my best shot but in 1948 I decided to call it quits, shook off the rain and headed home to the ranch. Pa always said, "When you can hear your neighbor's rooster crow, it's time to move on." There were just too many roosters crowin' in New York.

Pa didn't much care that I'd come home. I was just a girl. He probably didn't want me snoopin' into his private life though, because it was too easy talkin' him out of ten thousand dollars, enough to start a children's apparel shop in Rapid City. I wasn't the only one he loaned money to, either. Hokie Anderson and his brother Laverne, longtime friends and cattle dealers called Pa and told him they needed ten thousand dollars. "Sure, come on down," Pa said. When the men got to the ranch Pa asked, "Well, how much do you need?" Hokie knew it was a long shot to ask Pa for so much money. Pa got up from his chair and went over to the heavy black safe he once used in the Scenic Bank. The safe was encircled with a heavy chain and padlock. Pa opened the padlock, fiddled with the combination on the safe, and the door swung open. "Ten thousand? Well, God," Pa said sarcastically, "I thought you wanted some money!" He reached into the safe and pulled out a magazine. "Count out how much you need," he told Hokie. Between the pages of the magazine and in the pages of a large pile of other magazines within the dark safe Hokie took out ten thousand but he couldn't help noticing at least $190,000 more!

Goin' over the pass.

With the money Pa gave me I opened my shop and moved into Mama's home in town. I hadn't been there a month when early one morning the doorbell rang. I finally woke up enough to get the door open and there stood Hazel, the cook at the Circle Bar. With compressed mouth and snapping eyes she said, "I quit!"

"What's the matter Hazel?"

"I ain't agonna say, but I quit!"

"Well, Hazel, in the old days Pa used to chase 'em around the kitchen."

"He still does! I quit!"

Pa was a mere eighty-four years old at the time. That certainly cleared up the mystery of Mama's turnover in hired help.

Since Pa had arthritis pretty bad, especially in his knuckles, I came down to help cook until we could find another hired woman. I helped out with the cattle and was with him one day at the Keliher Place when he reached over to shut the gate with his painfully swollen hand. A bumblebee buzzed down and stung Pa right on his arthritic knuckle! He yelled and cussed up a storm. The next morning when he woke up the arthritis in his knuckle was completely gone! It seemed like a miracle. Ray experimented using bee venom, scraping a patch of raw flesh from Pa's arm, applying bee venom directly into the flesh. It burned like hell! After several applications over a period of two months, Pa never had arthritis again. At least one form of arthritis can be cured by bumblebee venom.

While I was still on the ranch people came around asking for donations from Pa for one thing or another. To look at Pa a person would've never known he had money. There were holes in his old cowboy boots and whenever he'd lose a button, he'd just staple his shirt or jacket together! His approach to giving money was simple. People asked for money for the damndest things. There were so many men with great ideas and lots of enthusiasm. Boy, they were going to do this and they were going to do that. Pretty soon they reached half their goal and the idea petered out. All the collected money donated toward the project went right down the drain! Pa's philosophy of giving was, "I'll give you the last five hundred (or one thousand) you'll need. You can count on it." If they carried through with their project, which was rare, and they were sincere, Pa's promised donation was worth something. Pa guaranteed the last payment and nobody ever went to Las Vegas with his money.

A neighbor who never borrowed money from Pa but earned quite a bit working for him over many years, Herman Bloom, was on the ranch one day when Pa demonstrated that he didn't always think making a buck more important than pride. A man from Belgium came to buy buckin' broncs for a rodeo. Pa put him on a little bay horse, but the "furriner" wasn't impressed at all. He screwed up his face and said, "Is that the best your horses can do?" Pa knuckled his mustache and Herman instantly backed away from the men. Pa glided up in front of the horse and went to fiddlin' with the halter while he talked to the man. With an almost invisible movement, Pa took a knife from his pocket and cut the jaw strap that controlled the horse's head. "Well, now, you jes' lope 'im right out through

No brakes — 1957.

that gate there an' he might do a little better," Pa told the man. By this time Herman knew enough to get up on the fence. The little "furriner" dug his spurs in hard and he'd hardly passed the gate when Herman saw the man sail straight up, and it was a hell of a long time before he came down.

Herman wanted to kill Pa on more than one occasion. He was comin' back to the ranch one afternoon after gettin' caught in a blizzard with temperatures thirty degrees below zero. He passed a hay field and one of Pa's young hired hands was out in the cold half dead, the tears on his cheeks frozen. "Billy," Herman yelled. "What the hell are you doin' out here?"

"Pete made me."

Herman wrapped the boy up, put him in the car, and headed for the ranch. As they got closer to the place, Herman got madder and madder. "That damn Pete would have worked the boy to death if I hadn't found him," Herman recalled. "I made up my mind I was goin' to face Pete and quit! Just as I got the boy up to the gate, here comes Pete to help, all apologetic saying in the most believable way, 'God Almighty Herman, if I'd know'd it was this cold, I'd never sent the kid out in it!' I didn't quit but I could've killed him anyway."

When Pa was nearly ninety years old Herman had the constant misfortune to have to ride along with him in the jeep. Pa loved his jeep because it was the closest thing to a horse he'd ever had. Of course, after six months the brakes were all worn out. He had a habit of turning left into the other lane when someone came by going the other way. Pa wanted to see who it was drivin' the other car! He scared people half to death. He was drivin' my car one day in eight inch ruts on a dirt road when he met another car coming fast from the opposite direction in the same ruts! Just as the other car ripped through, Pa jumped over his two passengers in the front seat and didn't get a scratch but my Ford coupe was turned into a pickup truck!

One of Pa's favorite tricks was takin people on hair-raising rides in his jeep. Herman remembered when it was his turn:

One afternoon it was gettin' late and we were headed for the ranch. It finally dawned on me that we were headed straight over a big high bluff! "Pete!" I says, "Pete, where the hell you goin'?"

"Well God, I'm goin' home," Pete said calmly. We got closer and I knew it was going to be a straight fall down hundreds of feet with no brakes.

"Well you ain't goin' over that bluff, are you?" I yelled at him. "Pete your lucks been good for a hundred and twenty-five years and mine ain't worth a damn! I'm bailin' out!" Just as we got to the edge, I bailed!

Lookin back Pete thundered, "Oh God Herman, it's the fella that bails out that gets hurt!" The jeep lurched forward over the bluff and as he went over, he gave a loud 'Whoop!' and went straight

Branding

*down that bluff. Sure, enough, I was the only one bruised and I
know I went the way of many."*

Pa's tricks played out for a time in 1955. Taxes were always a flea under his collar. The Internal Revenue Service finally caught up with him but he absolutely refused to talk to them about it. Ray ended up having to pay $110,000 to get the IRS off Pa's back! Pa had forty-three thousand deeded acres and he sure hated to part with a cent for taxes. That was what probably precipitated the heart attack.

Pa, Big Chuck, six cowboys, and I were rounding up steers. I got breakfast for the hands in the middle of the night and then we started over Sheep Mountain. As Pa came up at the beginning of the pass there was a steep rocky bank and his horse stumbled and jarred him. From then on I noticed he bent over in the saddle. By the time I got up to the top of the mountain, Pa was off his horse tryin' to throw up on the ground. Big Chuck half carried him back down the long steep pass and put him into the vehicle for the long bumpy ride back to the ranch. When I got him into bed and called Ray, I knew it was a heart attack. Pa hated hospitals and he was never in one very long. The nurse's got one look at his loaded .45 automatic and they'd raise the roof!

Of course, that didn't stop Pa but it slowed him down. He went to live with Myretta and Ray to recuperate but he didn't last long there. One day when he wasn't feeling good he asked Myretta, "Do you think I'll have to go to hell on top of all this?"

"No, Pete," she answered. "Grace will reach down and pull you up!" The man who was worrying about going to hell never dreamed he'd one day be inducted into the South Dakota Hall of Fame.

Pa came to live with me and he hadn't been there long when he started hinting around that a Mrs. Shellito, an old "friend" of his was living with her daughter and the teenage grandchildren were driving her crazy. So I invited ninety year-old Mrs. Shellito to come home and live with Pa. She was practically blind but as strong as a horse and she could cook. He'd lead her around and she made delicious pies. They made a pair. She was still living with us when we hired a private nurse to look in on Pa at night. The buxom night nurse always had to be careful because every time she turned her back on Pa, he'd reach over and pinch her!

Meanwhile, I had remarried and was in the real estate business. My husband John Warren owned all the wreckers and the only ambulance service in Rapid City. Pa lived with us and he could walk up a flight of stairs for meals, but was carried by ambulance to the hospital for tests and x-rays. He always sat bolt upright with his cowboy hat on, covered by a blue blanket over his lap. Pa enjoyed the masculine companionship of the drivers who humored him with a little ride until they got a call. Then they'd bring him home, siren blaring, and proceed on their way.

South end of Sheep Mountain—

Resting at waterhole.

The Badlands Fox—Pete Lemley.

A few weeks before Pa died in June 1961, my husband John was driving the ambulance. Pa was going to the hospital for an x-ray when John got an emergency call over the radio and he looked back at Pa and asked him if he was up to a fast ride to pick up a heart patient. Pa was delighted. Siren screaming, red lights flashing, cars pulled over to let the ambulance pass. The fancy stores on Main Street had just closed and pedestrians emptied onto the sidewalks, hurrying home to dinner and the Ed Sullivan Show. Pa blinked his sharp, blue eyes.

The streets became suddenly blurred with oxen teams pullin' heavy wagons of wood, ladies in big flowered hats walked demurely along the wooden boardwalk, fancy buggies with beautiful teams trotted past, and the streets bustled with the sounds of carpenters, horses, and happy children. Indian women in shawls pulled tightly over their partially hidden faces turned away as Pa looked up at the long white balcony of the stately Schnasse Dry Goods Building, filled with parasoled ladies waving lace handkerchiefs at the sight of a fearless, crusty fox leanin' out the window with his cowboy hat held high in the air bellowin,' "Let 'er Rip!" as the ambulance tore down the street.

Wild friends in the rafters of the barn.

Baby bottle orphans.

About the Author

Margaret Lemley Warren has been ranching solo since 1962 at the mouth of
Spring Creek on the Cheyenne River, close to
where Pete Lemley established his first horse ranch in the 1890s.

(Below) Shatzi.

A work day on the ranch.

*(Right)
"Save
the Doves."
1980*